The Lost Treasure
of the Golden Sun

Carol J. Amato

STARGAZER
Publishing Company
PO Box 77002
Corona, CA 92877-0100
"Educate, Enlighten, Empower"

Dedication

For Dylan and Justin and their new baby brother-to-be

Author's Note

American Sign Language does not have the same grammar and syntax as English; however, for readers to understand what the characters are signing, the language is represented using standard English.

Published by Stargazer Publishing Company
PO Box 77002
Corona, CA 92877-0100
(800) 606-7895
(951) 898-4619
FAX: (951) 898-4633
Corporate e-mail: stargazer@stargazerpub.com
Orders e-mail: orders@stargazerpub.com
www.stargazerpub.com
www.phantomhunters.com

Edited by Jeanne Lazo

Cover design by Michael Wheary and Matt Frantz

ISBN: 0-933277-01-7 (English, Hardcover)
ISBN: 0-9713756-5-8 (English, Softcover)
ISBN: 0-9713756-3-1 (Spanish, Softcover)

LCCN: 2004117661

Chapter 1

Intense heat rushed over Anny Bradford as if she had opened the door to a hot oven. Flames flashed before her, and she shrank against the vinyl upholstery of the old green station wagon as it rolled up the desert highway of the Navajo Nation. *Oh, no! Please! Not now!* She clutched her stomach, trying to ward off the image.

Flames crackled viciously, though she knew no one else in the car could see or hear them. Above the blaze floated a turquoise stone rimmed in silver on a beaded leather band. Smoke seared her lungs, sucking the air right out of them. She coughed violently, gasping for breath.

Beside her on the back seat, Scout nudged her and whispered, "You're not having another vision, are you?"

Anny ignored her twin. The flames began to lick at her. She raised her arms to protect herself against the blast as smoke stung her eyes.

"Don't let Jim see you," Scout continued, her tone more than a little irritated. "He'll send us home!"

Anny tried to control herself. Their parents and Eric Larson's grandma had let them fly alone to Arizona yesterday

1

from their homes in California. Not many twelve-year-olds got to do that. She didn't want to be responsible for ruining their first parent-free vacation.

Eric reached across Scout's lap to touch Anny's arm. He rapidly formed words with his hands, his way of talking because he was deaf. *"What are you seeing?"*

Anny wanted to sign back but couldn't. Sweat beaded on her forehead despite the chill that ran up her spine. She knew the leather band and flames weren't really there, yet she reached out to grasp the stone. As her fingers closed around it, the silver at its edges burned her skin. Pulling her arm back quickly, the stone still in her closed fist, she rolled down the window, desperately hoping that fresh air would save her. She thrust her burning hand outside and hurled the stone and band to the ground, gasping again as clean air replaced the smoke in her lungs. She prayed the experience would end.

"Hey! Roll it up!" cried Ben Lapahie from the front seat. "That wind is cold!" His coal-black eyes stared at her.

The driver, Ben's uncle, Jim Roanhorse, glanced at her in the rearview mirror. "What's wrong?" Without waiting for an answer, he pulled off the road and stopped.

Anny opened the door and stumbled out, leaning against the car for support. Scout was right behind her. Anny heard the other doors open.

Jim put a hand on Anny's shoulder. "What happened?"

"She'll be fine," Scout said quickly as Eric and Ben gaped. Scout moved between Anny and Jim. "This happens sometimes. It's nothing."

As the experience subsided, Anny breathed deeply. She examined her hands. No burns. She moved slightly so she could see Scout's face. Scout had the same exasperated look Mom got when Anny told her about the things she sensed. Scout never really made fun of her, but she wasn't very supportive, either. Just because they both shared the same long blond hair and brown eyes, people thought they must have the same interests and abilities, too. They didn't. Scout was the outdoorsy one who was popular, suntanned, and good at all things athletic, and who had been obsessed with Girl Scouts since becoming a Daisy at five.

Anny was different, very different. She wasn't good at sports and she wasn't outdoorsy—and she saw things that other people didn't. Determined to show everyone that she was normal, too, she studied hard and got good grades, something Scout didn't have an easy time doing.

"Looks like an anxiety attack to me," said Jim.

"Yeah...that's probably it," Scout agreed as Ben and Eric continued to stare. "Three of us in the back seat and all...."

Anny knew from past experience that this was no anxiety attack.

Chapter 2

"So you've had this before?" Jim asked.

Anny shot Scout and Eric a look she hoped said, "Don't say anything!" Then she nodded to Jim, feeling her cheeks flush. Many times she had seen things other people didn't. She had told her parents and other adults about her visions. They hadn't believed her. At first Mom had told her, "You just have an overactive imagination."

Mom's reaction to the last incident had been different. The neighbors had lost their pampered Siamese cat. While everyone was out looking for it, Anny had seen a vision of it in another neighbor's garage. She had told the owners to look there. She was happy to have been helpful, but instead of being thanked, she had gotten blamed for hiding the animal. "This is the only possible explanation," the neighbors had insisted, and her parents had agreed. Mom, a psychologist, had grown stern. "It looks like the neighbors are right, Anny. Whatever made you do such a thing?"

Mom became convinced that these "episodes," as she called them, meant there was something very wrong with Anny.

This had started an endless round of trips to a variety of doctors from psychologists to those who dealt with brain disorders to find out just what that "something" was. A few had pronounced her delusional, others a liar. Even Jordan, her ten-year-old brother, said she was crazy.

But Anny had known exactly what she had seen. *My experiences aren't my imagination! They have a meaning, and so does this one today, even if I don't understand what it is.* A lump rose in her throat as the pain of her family's thinking she was a liar overwhelmed her once again. The only ones who had ever believed her were Eric and her grandpa. Eric knew what it was like to be different, and Grandpa always told her that it was her "intuition" at work. He had gotten into more than a few heated discussions with her parents over her visits to the doctors. "There's nothing wrong with her," he always insisted. "You just don't understand her. Try to be more patient."

Anny struggled to calm down. She didn't dare tell Jim the truth. Better he thought she was homesick than to think she had mental problems. "I'm fine," she said, climbing back into the car. She could still feel the heat of embarrassment in her cheeks. "Let's go."

"You're sure?" Jim asked, obviously not convinced.

She nodded, avoiding his gaze.

"Okay, then.... We have a science fair to plan. Mrs. Nakai is waiting."

Ben, their family friend, had told Jim that Anny, Scout, and Eric, their next-door neighbor, had won first place in the middle-school division of their county science fair. Jim was a science teacher and Anny's dad's former college roommate. Jim had invited them to the Navajo Nation to help him and Mrs. Nakai, the principal, plan a science fair at their school. Anny and the others had been thrilled. Jim had promised their parents that the trip would be educational and safe—he'd see to it.

Anny was grateful he hadn't made a big deal out of her "anxiety attack." She really liked him. He and Ben were Navajos. They both had black eyes and hair, but Ben's hair was short, while Jim's fell down his denim jacket to the middle of his back. He also wore a big silver buckle on his belt and real cowboy boots.

In the car, Eric brushed his light-brown hair from his forehead, then signed to Anny, *"Tell me what happened."* His normally twinkling blue eyes looked worried.

"Later," she signed back. Fascinated by his ability to speak with his hands, Anny had convinced her mother to let her take sign language lessons. While not as fast as Eric, she was proud to be skilled enough to carry on real conversations. Eric was happy that she could sign. It made them even closer friends.

As they drove, Anny tried to forget her most recent "episode." Instead, she focused on the flat-topped, red mountains that towered above the desert floor beneath the cloudless blue sky. Dry, cool air whirled around her face through the window, which she left slightly open—just in case. Only towering cacti and short, scrubby bushes dotted the seemingly endless sandy landscape.

"Windy Mesa's just up ahead," Jim said, as they passed a slow-moving truck.

"Can you believe it's our vacation and we're going to *school*?" joked Scout.

Anny and the others laughed.

Jim turned the station wagon off the highway onto a dirt road. Anny grasped the armrest and the edge of her seat as the old car bounced and jolted over deep ruts. The uneasiness she had felt just before seeing the flames returned. She squeezed her eyes shut, trying to ward it off.

"Hey, look!" Ben pointed out the front window with his finger slightly bent. He had once told Anny that his people considered it rude to point straight at anyone.

Anny gritted her teeth, then squinted into the distance. A red fire truck, an old, faded blue pickup, and some cars were parked in front of a low, gray concrete building. Several men in tan uniforms stood beside the cars in front of open, wrought-iron gates, over which hung a sign: "Windy Mesa School."

"They're Tribal Police officers," said Jim.

The officers were talking with two men in jeans and cow-boy hats and a dark-haired woman in black pants and a red sweater. The woman shook her head as she listened, her arms crossed.

"That's Mrs. Nakai." Jim stopped the station wagon next to a white car with the words "Navajo Tribal Police" painted in large black letters on the door.

"Mr. Roanhorse!" The woman hurried around to Jim's side of the car, tears running down her face. "You're here!"

Jim opened the door and stepped out. "What's going on?"

"A fire—two days ago." Her voice shook. "Several class-rooms were destroyed, including your lab."

"What? I don't see anything burned."

The others scrambled out of the car. Anny swallowed hard, rooted to her seat as shock radiated from the top of her head to the ends of her fingertips and toes.

"I'll show you." Mrs. Nakai led the others through the wrought-iron gates.

Anny slowly opened the car door and got out. Just as slowly, she walked to the gates and peered beyond. The school was U-shaped, with the gates at the open end of the U. Scout and the others stood in a large courtyard filled with tables and benches.

Anny stared in stunned disbelief at the charred, black section in the back. There had been a fire *here*. The vision had not been her imagination. Her experience had been real, and she felt to the core of her bones that the two were connected. But how?

Chapter 3

Anny approached the group and watched as Jim craned his neck to see through the broken windows of a classroom, then threw his arms in the air. "My lab! Everything's ruined! The science projects, the microscopes, the equipment...!"

"I know, I know." The principal wrung her hands. "At first, the Sheriff thought it might have been caused by a loose wire or a faulty heater, but the investigators didn't find either one. They sent for an arson dog from a department in New Mexico. This fire was deliberately set."

Jim's eyes widened. "Someone *deliberately* did this?"

Mrs. Nakai put her hands to her face and nodded as tears trickled down her cheeks. "I have a hard time believing it myself. What if the kids had been here?"

Jim shuddered. "Don't even think about it. But who would do this? And *why*?"

"One of the investigators asked me if there was an angry employee or student, but I can't think of anyone."

"I can't either."

Mrs. Nakai let out a deep sigh. "Kids, I'm afraid we'll have to cancel our meeting for now."

"That's okay," said Scout.

It was fine with Anny. She was still too disturbed to think about a science fair anyway.

Eric stood by a pile of rubble in front of the burned classrooms. He motioned for her to come over to him, then pointed to a rock with a bright-yellow sun, reddish-brown horses, and other animals painted on it. Unlike the rocks around it, which were charred black, this rock was unbelievably clean.

"That's impossible!" she exclaimed. "Hey, Ben! Come here!"

Ben broke away from his conversation with Mrs. Nakai and ran over to them as the others followed. "What?"

Eric could also read lips and speak. He pointed again to the small boulder and said, "The fire didn't touch it." He had learned to speak words that he could not hear, and because of that, his pronunciation had a different rhythm. His words sounded muffled, though understandable.

Mrs. Nakai looked closely at the stone and seemed surprised. "The Magic Rock! I forgot all about it."

"Magic Rock?" asked Anny.

"Yes. Archaeologists found it in the desert when I was a little girl. Instead of putting it in a museum, they brought it to this school for good luck."

"The colors on that rock should have faded hundreds of years ago," said Jim. "They didn't, and that's how the rock got its name."

"It was displayed in a clear plastic box in the hallway," Mrs. Nakai explained. "I wonder how it got out here...?"

Jim kicked at shards of clear material on the ground. "Here's what's left of the plastic box."

"And the Magic Rock has something to do with buried treasure," added Ben.

"Buried treasure?" Anny and Scout repeated.

"That's just an old legend," Jim said.

"Can we look for it anyway?" asked Anny.

Jim shook his head. "There's no truth to that story. Anyway, treasure-hunting on the reservation is illegal."

"It is?" Scout sounded disappointed. "Why?"

"There are historical artifacts everywhere, not to mention the bones of people who were buried centuries ago. Some are our ancestors."

Just as disappointed, Anny pointed to the stone's pictures. "What are those?"

"Pictographs," Jim explained. "That's a fancy word for rock paintings. The Anasazi made them."

"Anasazi?" asked Scout.

"The Ancient Ones," explained Mrs. Nakai. "They lived here before our people came and disappeared around the year 1500. Archaeologists think they ran out of food because of a long drought."

"Look!" Scout pointed to the pile of rubble. "There's a big hole in the ground."

Anny leaned over for a closer look. Sure enough, next to the rock and almost hidden from sight under the concrete foundation of the school was a large hole. *I'm no expert*, Anny thought, *but that looks freshly dug.*

"Be careful," Mrs. Nakai warned. "The firefighters told me about that. I can't imagine how it got there."

"Somebody was obviously digging under here," said Jim, "but I can't even begin to guess why."

Two men in cowboy hats entered the courtyard. Anny felt the strange uneasiness again. She swallowed hard. The men were the same ones talking to the police earlier. One man was short and chubby, and scraggly strands of dirty, brown hair stuck out from a dusty gray hat pulled down to shade his eyes. The other was tall and thin with a dark, neatly trimmed beard and gold wire-rimmed glasses. Around the brim of his hat was a multicolored, beaded headband with a large turquoise stone in the front.

Anny stumbled backwards as the two men walked toward the group. *That headband is just like the one in my vision!*

"What's wrong now?" Scout whispered to her.

Anny shook her head, unable to speak. She quickly tried to recover herself so that no one would notice her reaction.

The tall man pushed his hat back on his head, revealing thick brows. His dark eyes narrowed as he faced the principal. "The firefighters say it's okay to go into those burned classrooms now. You'll need help sifting through everything to see what you can save. We'd like to volunteer to help."

"But won't you be busy on your archeological dig?"

"Archaeological dig?" Scout exclaimed. "Can we see it?"

No! Anny cried silently, though she really didn't know why. She wished they would go back to Jim's so she could curl up in a ball on her bed and think.

"Wonderful idea!" said Mrs. Nakai. "Dr. Philip Sanderson and Bill Thomas are from the University of Arizona."

"My old school," said Jim.

Dr. Sanderson's eyes widened. "Really...?"

Jim held out his hand. "I've heard about you. You've done a lot of important work here."

Dr. Sanderson shook Jim's hand but said nothing.

Mrs. Nakai introduced everyone, then said to the two archaeologists, "These children won their county science fair in California and came here to help us plan one of our own. I'm sure they'd learn a lot from seeing your dig."

Dr. Sanderson glanced at his partner with what almost looked like some type of signal.

Anny noticed a jagged scar running from the chubby man's right eye down his cheek to his chin.

Dr. Sanderson cleared his throat. "I suppose.... We should be set up...maybe tomorrow or the next day."

"Where is it?" asked Jim.

"Uh...over by Calico Mesa." He turned to Mrs. Nakai. "Helping you won't be a problem, though, Ma'am."

"We'll help, too," offered Ben.

Dr. Sanderson cleared his throat again. "That's okay. It's dangerous in there. You don't want to get hurt."

Anny sighed with relief. Maybe they would be leaving for Jim's soon, after all.

"It'll take more than just the two of you to go through this mess," said Jim. "We'll be happy to help out, won't we, kids? Besides, I want to see what I can salvage from my lab."

So much for wishing, Anny thought. She'd just have to muster her courage.

"Thank you all so much," said Mrs. Nakai. "We can start now, if that's okay with everyone."

For several hours, the men helped Mrs. Nakai haul out large pieces of gritty carpet, along with the charred remains of desks, chairs, and tables. They piled all of it in front of the school. Anny and the other kids sorted through the blackened, soggy stacks of papers and books.

"I never realized schoolrooms had so much stuff!" Scout said, her hands covered in soot.

Jim groaned. "What will the kids say when they have to start their science projects all over?"

Anny knew how devastated she would feel if this had happened to her.

Mrs. Nakai let out a deep sigh. "The budgets are stretched to the maximum. I don't know how we'll afford to rebuild the classrooms now—or replace all the books and equipment."

Jim shook his head slowly. "You're right. It'll cost fifty to a hundred thousand dollars at least...."

"*Fifty to a hundred thousand dollars?*" cried Anny.

Mrs. Nakai nodded. "Maybe more. That's money we just don't have."

When they finished, Dr. Sanderson and Bill headed for their truck. Jim carried the Magic Rock to Mrs. Nakai's office for safekeeping.

"I'll let you know when we can meet about the science fair," the principal told the kids as they walked back to the car. "I feel so awful. You came all this way to talk about it, and you've ended up cleaning a mess instead."

"That's okay," said Anny, and the others agreed.

Mrs. Nakai brushed dust from her black pants. "You've been wonderful. The job was so much easier to handle."

"We'll be here until next Sunday morning," Anny told her, trying to be polite as she braced herself against another wave of uneasiness. "There's plenty of time."

"We can still plan a really good one," Eric said aloud.

An engine coughed and sputtered. Dr. Sanderson and Bill sat in the dusty, blue pickup, its windows rolled down.

"Try it again," Anny heard Bill say.

Ben was at the driver's door in no time. "Having trouble? Maybe I can start your truck for you."

Dr. Sanderson poked his head out the window in surprise. "Yeah? This old thing has been acting up lately."

"I help out in my cousin's garage. It might be just a loose wire." Ben moved around to the front of the truck. "Pull the hood lever. I'll take a look."

With a loud click, the hood latch released.

Ben propped the hood open and leaned over the engine. Shortly, he stood up and yelled, "Try it now."

Dr. Sanderson turned the key in the ignition. The engine still coughed and sputtered.

Ben released the rod holding up the hood, let the hood slam shut, and walked to the driver's door. "Can I try?"

Dr. Sanderson stared at him a moment, then shrugged and traded places with Ben.

The engine sputtered a few times, then began to hum.

"Can I drive it across the parking lot just to check it out?" Ben said out the window.

Dr. Sanderson eyed him suspiciously. "*You* can drive?"

"Sure. My cousin taught me."

"Out here, kids learn young," Jim explained. "It's okay so long as they stay off the main roads."

Dr. Sanderson stepped back. "Be my guest."

Gears shifted, and with a jerk, the truck rolled forward.

"Ben said he knew a lot about cars, but he never mentioned knowing how to drive," Anny exclaimed as Scout and Eric watched open-mouthed.

The truck rolled to a stop. The gears shifted again, and Ben looked out the rear window and backed up to where he had started.

Opening the door, he jumped out. "It was a loose wire like I thought, but your truck sure could use a lot of work."

"I know." The archaeologist sounded upset. "No time to buy a new one right now. Just hope the old heap lasts until we're done." He climbed into the cab. "Thanks, kid!" he called as he and Bill drove off.

Jim opened the door to the station wagon. "My dad should be at my house. He wants to meet all of you. He'll be shocked to hear what's happened."

On the way to Jim's house, Anny thought about the fire and her vision. *Why do these things happen to me? What do they mean? And if they do mean something, what good are they when no one believes me anyway?*

Finally, a house appeared up ahead. A huge tree with gnarled limbs towered over the long, low peach-colored stucco dwelling. With its overhanging porch and deep green western-style posts and rails, Jim's place seemed like an oasis.

Jim pulled into the driveway beside a new red pickup. Anny knew he had borrowed the station wagon from his father so he would have room to drive all of them around. In the meantime, his father was using Jim's truck.

Inside, Jim's father was sewing beads onto a leather belt at the counter that separated the small kitchen and eating area from the living room. Jim introduced everyone to him, and Anny was fascinated by his work. Mr. Roanhorse looked like Jim, except for his lined face and graying hair, which hung in two long braids. He wore a red-and-yellow flowered, loose-fitting shirt with a red sash tied around his waist.

When he heard about the fire at the school, Mr. Roanhorse stopped working, put his leatherwork into a green and blue woven cloth bag, and looked up. "An evil spirit follows the person who would do such damage." His eyes never left Anny's as he spoke.

Chapter 4

Anny's skin crawled. *Why is he looking at me? Does he think I had something to do with the fire?*

Mr. Roanhorse must have noticed her discomfort, for he smiled at her as if he understood her feelings. His emotions seemed to get right inside her to soothe her mind and soul. The trauma of the morning's event faded, and she didn't feel like curling up in a ball anymore.

"How about some roasted corn-on-the-cob and fry bread?" Jim said, interrupting her thoughts. He pulled out a large silver pot from a shelf under the counter and began filling it with water from the sink.

"What's fry bread?" asked Scout.

He set the pot on the stove. "Navajo bread fried in a skillet. It's round like a tortilla but thicker. You'll like it."

"Can I help?" Scout asked Jim. "I love to cook."

"That would be great." He retrieved a dented, black frying pan from another cupboard.

"Right after I call my mom to let her know what happened." Scout turned to Anny. "Can I have the phone?"

Anny reached into her backpack for the cell phone and handed it to her sister. Envying the closeness Scout had with their mother, she wished she could share in it. That was just a dream, though, she realized with a twinge of sadness.

As Jim set about boiling the corn with Scout at his elbow, Anny noticed Eric in the living room studying a painting hanging over the brown leather couch. He obviously wanted to talk.

She glanced at Ben. He was speaking to his grandfather. She took the opportunity to tell Eric what happened. He would believe her. *"I could feel the smoke in my throat and the flames burning my skin! I had to open the window to toss the headband out and get some fresh air so I could breathe."*

"I knew it was something real bad," he signed back. *"It could be a...premonition. I think that's what it's called. Except a premonition usually happens before the real thing does."* He paused. *"We'll talk more later. Let's pretend we're talking about this painting."*

Anny nodded, grateful that she had someone to confide in. When she got home, she would tell Grandpa, too. He always had comforting things to say. Unlike her parents, he helped her find a meaning for her experiences.

The painting pictured a desert scene. In the middle was a wall of tan, smooth rock with an arched top and a gaping hole in its center. The unusual formation fascinated Anny. She moved closer to study it. "It's beautiful," she said and signed.

"My dad painted that," Ben called from across the room.

"It's Window Rock," added Jim. "The capital of the Navajo Nation got its name from that formation."

Scout joined them. "It looks like someone used a giant ice cream scoop to take out the center!"

Jim fiddled with the knobs on the stove. "The wind and rain did that. We'll try to go there this week so you can see it for real."

Anny signed their words for Eric.

"I'd like to get a picture of that!" he said.

"While we're here, I'll do some drawing," Ben said.

Anny knew he hoped to be like his father, a famous artist in Phoenix, where the family lived. She herself couldn't decide whether to be a scientist-astronaut or a mystery writer.

"Time to set the table." Opening a drawer, Jim pulled out several knives, forks, and spoons with bright-yellow plastic handles.

"I'll do that," Anny offered.

Soon a sweet aroma filled the room.

Later, as they sat around the table, Anny had to admit she hadn't tasted anything quite like the golden pieces of frybread. Some were covered in cinnamon, others in butter and honey. Anny decided she loved their sweet flavor.

After the table was cleared and the dishes washed, Jim said, "Since we can't work on the science fair, how about going to my dad's hogan for a few days?"

"What's a hogan?" Anny asked.

"A traditional Navajo house—a small eight-sided home made of logs. Dad lives in one about an hour away."

"What can we do there?" asked Scout.

"Ride horses, for one thing."

"All right!" Scout shouted. "I already have my Horse Lover and Horseback Rider badges."

"Then let's go to the trading post and pick up some supplies," said Jim.

Mr. Roanhorse pulled a wide-brimmed black felt hat from the hall closet.

Anny stopped short when she saw the colorful beaded band around the crown. It was like Dr. Sanderson's, but without the pretty turquoise stone in the front. Now she was even more confused about her vision earlier that day. *Did it relate to Dr. Sanderson or Mr. Roanhorse? Both? Neither?* She thought about this as they went outside.

"Can we ride in the back of your pickup?" asked Ben.

"It isn't safe. Ride in Grandfather's car with him."

As they followed Jim's pickup down the road, Anny looked across the vast sandy land. "The desert seems to go on forever," she thought out loud. "It's as though the only things here besides us are all those scrubby bushes."

"And all those creepy crawlies," teased Ben.

Anny winced in disgust. "Yuck!" She felt Scout's elbow jab her side.

"Don't be a baby."

A half-hour later, they parked on a gravel lot in front of a small building. Made of vertical wooden planks painted a deep red, it had two large windows on either side of its double-door entry. Its porch had the same style posts and rails as those on Jim's house. A sign above the porch's overhang read, "Red Rock Trading Post" in faded black letters.

"That looks just like something right out of a cowboy movie!" Scout's heels clacked on the boardwalk.

Entering the darkened building, Anny blinked, trying to adjust to the change in light. She ran her fingers over the tan baskets and the smooth black, red, and white pottery that stacked the shelves. Rough woven rugs with multi-colored designs hung on the walls and gave off the smell of rope.

While the boys began looking over shelves of groceries and tools, Anny and Scout stopped at a glass case to admire the silver jewelry. It held some of the same bright turquoise stones she had seen on Dr. Sanderson's hat. Anny immediately noticed a silver bracelet with a turquoise stone in the middle and zigzag designs carved on the band.

"Look at this cool necklace." Scout pointed to a silver and turquoise star on a thin silver chain. "I want that."

Tires crunched over the gravel outside. Anny turned to look. A familiar blue pickup truck drove past the windows and disappeared around the side of the building. *That looks just like Dr. Sanderson's old rattletrap.* Her uneasiness returned. Closing her eyes, she gripped her stomach. *Not again!*

She jumped as she felt a tap on her shoulder. It was Eric.

"Look at this cool yo-yo I bought."

She stared at the orange toy. *"You're at an Indian trading post and you bought a yo-yo?"*

"Why not? Want to watch me do some tricks?" He began to unwind the string.

"Magic tricks with a yo-yo?" Anny loved to watch Eric perform magic at school.

"No, just yo-yo tricks."

"I'm getting those funny feelings again...."

He stuffed the toy in his pocket. *"Let's go outside."*

Following him out onto the porch, Anny hugged a post, breathing deeply.

"Are you okay?"

Her uneasiness began to fade. *"I think so...."*

Eric looped the string on his finger. Hurling the yo-yo away from his hand, the orange wheel flew off into the dirt beyond the side of the porch. He jumped off the porch and scooped up the yo-yo, then stood up, staring straight ahead.

Before Anny could move, he was back on the porch, peering around the edge of the building and staring again.

Anny tapped him on the shoulder, but he held up his hand for her to wait. Then he pressed his finger against his lips and signed, *"Dr. Sanderson is over there talking to Bill. He said he thought the treasure was beneath the golden sun."*

"What treasure? The one Ben was talking about?"

Eric shrugged. *"He didn't say."*

"Are you sure that's what he said?"

"I could read his lips real plain from here. He also said 'Watch them. They're in our way.'"

Anny loved a good mystery. Pressing herself against the trading post wall, she peered around the corner. Dr. Sanderson and Bill stood next to their truck talking. Their faces were plainly visible. Eric's lip-reading teacher said he was the best student she had ever taught. There was no doubt that Eric was right.

23

Dr. Sanderson pulled a piece of paper from his pocket, unfolded it, and smoothed it out on the hood of the truck. He and Bill bent over it, studying it and conversing rapidly.

Anny turned back to Eric. *"I believe you. They're looking at a piece of paper. I'll bet it's a map. Maybe it's the map to the treasure."*

Eric put the yo-yo in his pocket. *"Do you remember the Magic Rock at the school? Maybe that's the treasure. It had that big yellow sun drawn on it."*

"You think Dr. Sanderson wanted to steal the rock?" She felt her cheeks flush with embarrassment at the thoughts of how people would react to that suggestion. *"Sounds crazy, doesn't it? Don't tell anyone."*

Eric frowned. *"What did he mean when he said, 'They're in our way'? Who's in their way?"*

Chapter 5

"I don't know." Anny grabbed Eric's arm and pulled him back inside the trading post. *"We should tell Jim."*

She signaled Scout and Ben to go over to the far corner where no one could see them, then touched Eric's arm so he would look at her. "Tell them what you saw," she prompted.

"Is anything wrong?" Jim came around the aisle with Mr. Roanhorse. Both had armloads of groceries.

"Dr. Sanderson is looking for treasure," said Anny. "You said nobody is supposed to be doing that."

Speaking aloud, Eric explained what he had seen.

Jim shifted the groceries in his arms. "That can't be what he meant. The only people who can get permits to dig are archaeologists like Dr. Sanderson. What they find is sent to museums and universities or is reburied where they found it. They don't keep anything for themselves."

"What about that treasure Ben talked about?" Eric asked. "Is that buried around here?"

Jim shrugged. "That's just a myth. Everyone knows there isn't anything to those stories. That's all they are—fairy tales. Don't fall for any of them."

"There is some truth in every legend, my son," said Mr. Roanhorse.

Anny stared at Ben's grandfather.

Jim frowned. "Now, Dad, don't go telling these kids those old stories."

"*Is* there a treasure?" prodded Anny.

"Yeah! *Is there?*" echoed Ben.

Mr. Roanhorse set his groceries on a shelf and sat down on a pile of brightly colored blankets stacked on top of a warped, weathered barrel. "A long time ago," he began, "when the Spanish were trying to take over this land, a soldier named Diego Garza stole a treasure of gold from them."

"Dad...," Jim said in disapproval.

Mr. Roanhorse glanced at his son, leaned forward, then pulled the wide brim of his black hat farther down over his forehead. "The treasure was very valuable," he continued. "Other Spaniards wanted it, and they followed Garza all over *Dinétah*—that's what we call our homeland. The legend says Garza buried the treasure here 'beneath the golden sun.' He buried his family's gold, jeweled cross with it so the other *conquistadores* wouldn't take it. They caught Garza, but he never told them where he buried the treasure."

"Beneath the golden sun...?" Eric repeated aloud. "That's what Dr. Sanderson said. He thought the treasure was beneath the golden sun, too. Is that the only thing Diego Garza said about where the treasure was?"

"The legend says a white man—I think he was a cowboy—discovered a map that Garza drew and followed it," Mr.

Roanhorse went on. "He got lost in the desert. When he was found, he claimed he located the treasure, but when he tried to tell people, his words were all jumbled up. No one could understand him. The legend says that a warrior guards the treasure and that he cast a spell on him." Mr. Roanhorse stood up and picked up his groceries. "That is the way the story was handed down from my father and his father before him."

"Why haven't you told me this before, Grandfather?" asked Ben. He didn't wait for an answer. "If 'beneath the golden sun' means the sun in the sky, the treasure could be anywhere!"

"Where would anyone even begin to look?" asked Scout.

"Dr. Sanderson thought he had an idea where," said Anny, as the kids followed Jim and his father toward the counter.

Jim pulled his wallet from his back pocket and paid the cashier. "I'm sure you've misinterpreted what he said. The University wouldn't send archaeologists—especially a famous one like Dr. Sanderson—to hunt for treasure without telling the Navajo Council. As I said, there are lots of those stories. The Lost Dutchman's Mine is the most famous." He took his change from the cashier. "Anyway, even if the legend were true, I'm sure someone stole the treasure long ago."

Jim and Mr. Roanhorse took the groceries out to the car, and Scout leaned back against the counter. "Well, guess you're wrong about Dr. Sanderson."

"He *said* he was looking for treasure," insisted Eric, aloud.

Anny thought again about her vision of the fire and the headband. "I believe Eric saw what he saw. Dr. Sanderson *is* looking for treasure."

"Why would he do that?" said Scout. "He'd be in real big trouble. It doesn't make sense."

Anny knew her suspicions about Dr. Sanderson were right. He obviously believed a treasure still existed—and she was sure her vision had something to do with it. *Ben's grandpa is right, too. Legends can be real.*

The kids piled into Mr. Roanhorse's station wagon. Anny saw the turquoise star hanging around Scout's neck and realized she hadn't bought anything. Too distracted by the thoughts of treasure and Dr. Sanderson and the fire, she hoped she would have another chance to shop for souvenirs.

As they pulled away from the trading post, she saw Dr. Sanderson and Bill watching them from beside their truck. Only when Jim had driven off the gravel onto the road did the two men head inside.

The sun was low in the sky when they arrived back at Jim's house. Anny filled her backpack with just enough clothes from her suitcase for their stay at the hogan. She packed her camera and the new hiking boots her parents had bought her and Scout just for this trip. Anny loved her boots, though she didn't like wearing the same clothes as her sister. Dressing differently was one way she let everyone know they had separate personalities.

As she shoved some film and her favorite red sweatshirt and jeans into the backpack, she thought again about Dr. Sanderson and Bill. *Why didn't they come into the trading post while we were inside? Why did they wait until we left? They must have been avoiding us.*

She had an idea. She glanced over at Eric, who was busy in the living room showing a card trick to Scout.

I can handle this for now, she told herself. She nudged Ben, who sat next to her stuffing his toothbrush and toothpaste into his backpack. "Doesn't your Aunt Elaine teach at the University of Arizona?"

"Yeah, she teaches biology. Why?"

"That's perfect!"

"For what?"

Anny glanced around, then whispered, "Let's e-mail her to see if she knows anything about Dr. Sanderson."

Ben groaned. "You still think he's treasure-hunting?"

"Let's just see what your aunt can find out. It'll only take a minute. Do you know her e-mail address?"

"Sure."

Anny grabbed the laptop off the couch. "Let's go for it!" Quickly she placed it on the kitchen table as Jim took food out of the refrigerator. "Okay if we use your telephone line to send an e-mail?" she asked him. Dad had promised Anny a wireless modem for winning the science fair, but they hadn't had a chance to shop for it yet.

"Of course." Jim closed the refrigerator door and packed the food into the cooler.

"Here's the stuff for the s'mores." Scout handed Jim graham crackers, chocolate bars, and marshmallows.

"Where'd that stuff come from?" asked Anny. "I didn't see you pack it."

Scout smiled. "Mom got them for us as a surprise."

Images of s'mores over a glowing fire flooded Anny's mind. She pushed them aside. She didn't want to make herself hungry, and she sure didn't want to bring back her vision of the fire. Swallowing hard to ward off any twinges of uneasiness, she slid into a chair, plugged the telephone cord into the outlet, flipped open the laptop lid, and logged on. She brought up the Compose Mail screen, then rose from the chair. "Okay, Ben, it's all yours."

"This is a waste of time," he grumbled, sitting down.

"Just send her a message. What harm can it do?"

Ben sighed. "What should I ask her?"

"Just say Dr. Sanderson's an archaeologist from her school. Ask her if she can find out what he's doing here."

Anny leaned over Ben's shoulder as his fingers flew rapidly over the keyboard. "Tell her to get back to us as soon as possible." Then she told Eric what they had done.

"Good idea. Can I e-mail my grandma? I want to tell her about the fire."

"Okay."

Eric had lived with his grandma since he was five, right after his parents were killed in a car accident. Luckily, he hadn't been in the car with them.

"It's Saturday night," Anny told Ben. "We probably won't hear back until tomorrow, so I'll bring the laptop."

Jim passed them carrying the cooler. "You won't need that out there. There's no electricity or phone lines."

Anny unplugged the modem cord and reattached Jim's phone. *"What?"*

Scout stopped packing. "You mean there's no TV?"

"TV? Who cares? What about my computer?"

Ben zipped his backpack. "Sorry. No toilets, either."

"Cool!" Scout slung her sleeping bag over her shoulder. "A real wilderness camp!"

Anny was frantic. "No way! We need to get on the Internet!" She slumped down into the chair. Without that wireless modem, she was tied to the telephone lines. They wouldn't be back from the hogan until Monday. She just knew Dr. Sanderson was hunting for treasure.

Chapter 6

Anny felt a poke in her arm.

"You're acting crazy," Ben whispered.

How many times have I heard that before? she thought. *Darn not having that wireless modem!*

"We don't know if we'll even hear from my aunt," Ben went on. "And even if we do, she may not know anything." He picked up his backpack. "Forget about it for now."

Anny wondered if Ben was right. *Maybe I* am *acting crazy. The treasure may not even exist at all.* She decided to vent by writing in her journal. Sitting back down at the computer, she opened a new file.

> *It's our first day at the Navajo Nation, and crazy me has done it again. I had another vision. I don't dare tell anyone. It's risky writing about it here. If Mom or Dad find this, they'll send me to the psychiatrist for sure. That fire and headband seemed so real. Not only that, I think some archaeologists are treasure-hunting. I'm probably as nuts as everybody says. Except Eric. He believes me. I love Scout, but she doesn't seem to understand me anymore.*

She stopped typing, sad that the closeness she had always shared with her twin was being disrupted by her strange experiences and her growing distance from her mother. The idea of losing that closeness scared her, and she vowed that, somehow, she would get herself, Scout, and her mom back on track. How she was going to do that she wasn't quite sure.

Shutting off the laptop, she decided to put all thoughts of her uneasy feelings, Dr. Sanderson, and lost treasure out of her head for now. *I'm going to learn to ride a horse this weekend, and that will be fun.*

In the living room, she packed everything she needed.

"Can opener, flashlight, knife, compass, wire, rope, sharpening stone, first aid kit—"

Anny looked up to see her twin reading from a piece of paper in one hand, a pencil poised above it in the other.

"What're you doing?" Ben asked, staring at Scout.

"Checking to see I have all my camping supplies."

"Why do you want to carry all that junk?" he scoffed. "You won't need any of it."

"A Girl Scout is always prepared," Scout returned, continuing to scan the paper. Then she looked at Ben. "I'm tired of people making fun of my Girl Scout stuff. One of these days, you'll find out how useful it is."

Anny laughed inwardly. Her sister never went anywhere without her Girl Scout equipment. That's how she had earned her nickname. Her real name was Rowan. Scout had just recently stopped wearing mostly Girl Scout clothes and started spending hours in the mall with Mom looking for "cute outfits." *Jeans and sweatshirts are just fine by me*, she told herself, but she knew it wasn't true.

Jim set their sleeping bags by the front door. "Shall we sleep inside the hogan or out?"

Anny raised her hand. "Inside!"

"No!" protested Scout. "Outside. It's much more fun!"

"Yeah!" agreed Ben.

Jim touched Eric's arm. "How about you? Shall we sleep inside the hogan or outside?"

"Outside," Eric answered.

"Looks like you're outvoted, Anny," said Jim. "Sorry."

Anny gave in. "Okay, okay."

The drive to the hogan took over an hour. Made of pine logs, the hogan had eight sides, just as Jim had described. Wisps of smoke floated in graceful ribbons from a tall pipe in the top of its curved, mud roof. Several horses milled in a corral. Wooly sheep roamed close by.

Anny grabbed her backpack from the floor under her feet and stepped from the car in the growing dusk.

"The door to a hogan faces east, so people inside can see the morning sun when they get up," explained Jim. "When you visit someone who lives in a hogan, it's polite to stand away from it until someone comes out to get you."

Scout removed her backpack from the rear of the station wagon. "Why?"

"Traditional Navajos like my father believe that evil spirits might be with you. It gives the spirits a chance to go away. But we all know there isn't any such thing."

Just then Mr. Roanhorse came through the low wooden door. "*Ya e'eh tey.*"

"That means 'hello,'" Jim explained.

"*Ya e'eh tey*," Jim and Ben answered.

"Come in, come in," said Mr. Roanhorse.

They followed him through the doorway. Dim light from kerosene lanterns filled the large open room inside. An old woman with long, gray braids stood by a black stove stirring something in a big pot. Like Mr. Roanhorse, she wore traditional Navajo clothes. A belt of round pieces of silver circled the waistline of her ankle-length red skirt. A necklace of silver beads with a big piece of silver in the middle stood out sharply against her purple velvet shirt. Anny thought she looked like a beautiful butterfly.

Grasping a section of her skirt, Mrs. Roanhorse used it as a potholder to open a door in the stove's front. Crackling fire glowed through the opening. She picked up a piece of wood from a basket on the floor, threw it into the fire, lifted a section of her skirt again and closed the door.

"This is my grandmother," said Ben, taking her hand.

The woman smiled, pointed to white sheepskins on the dirt floor, and said something in a language that Anny couldn't understand.

"She doesn't speak much English," Ben explained, as his grandmother began stirring again. "She wants us to sit down until dinner is ready."

They dropped their backpacks to the floor and sat on the soft sheepskins in the dim light. The hogan was about sixteen feet across, and several of its log walls had glass windows. Anny felt as if she were standing in a giant version of her par-ents' cedar closet. A table and chairs stood against one wall. Further along, a large loom, like one Anny had seen in a museum, held a bright red, yellow, and black partially completed weaving in a zigzag pattern. Against another wall was an iron bed covered with a thick blue-and-white-checkered comforter.

Later, over a meal of lamb, cornmeal, and more fry bread, Mr. Roanhorse told them how the Navajos had passed through three other worlds before emerging here in the Fourth, or Glittering, World. Anny thought their religion was fascinating. She couldn't wait to learn more about it on the Internet.

Scout brought out the chocolate bars, marshmallows, and graham crackers for the s'mores.

Jim rubbed his hands together. "You've had real Navajo food, so now let's see if we can get my parents to try real Girl Scout food!" He laughed.

"S'mores are great," Scout assured the Roanhorses.

The expressions on their faces told Anny they weren't so sure. "Should we really have them try these?" she asked Ben, who laughed and nodded.

The kids put marshmallows on the ends of long sticks Jim had brought and held them in the stove's fire.

Ben took two marshmallows off his stick and placed them over a chocolate bar that rested on a graham cracker. "Tell us more about the treasure, Grandfather."

Anny was surprised at his question. After all, he had told her she was acting crazy thinking about it.

Ben put another graham cracker over the marshmallows, lifted all of it up, and squeezed it tightly together to make the chocolate melt. "Where do you think it is?"

"That I do not know, Grandson."

"What would happen if we could find it?" asked Scout.

"I think there is a reward," said Mr. Roanhorse.

"How much?" asked Ben.

"Maybe...one hundred thousand dollars."

"One hundred thousand dollars?" all four kids exclaimed.

"Now, Dad, don't fill their heads with any more of this nonsense. Even if there is a reward, no one will ever collect it, because the treasure doesn't exist."

"Wouldn't it be great if it did and we could find it, though?" said Scout. "If I got that reward, I'd go to Girl Scout Camp *all* summer, buy tons of new clothes and a new telescope, and take my family to Europe."

"I'd buy tons of art supplies and get that easel I wanted and take art lessons in downtown Phoenix," said Ben, "and I'd go to Washington to see the National Museum of Art."

Eric signed as he talked. "I'd go to soccer camp and buy season tickets to the baseball, football, and soccer games for me and all my friends."

"Gee," said Anny, looking at him. "I thought you'd use it for college." Eric often talked of becoming a psychologist so he could help other kids who had lost their parents.

"I want to do that, too. I'd just want to spend some now."

The room fell silent. Then Ben turned to Anny. "What would you do with the reward?"

She thought a moment. "It came from the Navajo Nation. It should stay here. I would give it to Mrs. Nakai to rebuild the school and Jim's science lab."

"Yeah!" said Eric.

"Great idea!" said Scout.

"It sure is!" Ben handed his grandparents a s'more.

Mr. Roanhorse's gaze met Anny's, and she took it to mean he liked her idea about using the reward to help rebuild the school.

"Thanks for the generous thoughts, kids," Jim told them, "but I'm afraid it's just wishful thinking."

Mr. Roanhorse took a bite of the s'more. "Mm-mm, this is good," he said, and Mrs. Roanhorse nodded in agreement.

Though no one spoke of the treasure again while they finished their s'mores, Anny hoped she would get a chance to talk to Mr. Roanhorse about where it might be. She was enjoying watching him and Mrs. Roanhorse. It made her feel as though she were a real pioneer back in the old West. She wanted to take photos, but Jim had told her that traditional Navajos didn't like their pictures taken. They believed the photos captured part of their spirits. Anny kept her camera safely stowed in her backpack so no one would be offended.

"Well, kids," said Jim, "it's time for bed. We have a very long day tomorrow."

As everyone got up, Mrs. Roanhorse removed a coffee pot from the stove and said something to them in Navajo.

"What did she say?" Anny asked Ben.

"Never mind," said Jim.

38

"She said not to look around too much outside because we might see a ghost fire and that's bad luck," said Ben.

"A ghost fire? Are there ghosts around here?"

"You know there isn't any such thing," said Jim.

"You say that too quickly, my son," warned Mr. Roanhorse. He shook his head. "You disappoint me sometimes. You are blinded by the white man's ways. You know that I have seen such things myself. Heed your mother's words."

"Sorry, Dad. I didn't mean any disrespect. I just don't want the kids getting scared."

"Don't worry," said Scout. "We're not scared."

Anny wasn't sure whether to be afraid or not. Mr. Roanhorse said he had seen ghosts. She thought back over her past visions. Were some of them ghosts? Once, when she was in the park, she had sensed someone's eyes boring right through her. Whirling around, she had seen an elderly, gray-haired woman standing under a nearby tree. Sweetly, the lady had said, "How are you, Anny?" Anny hadn't recognized her nor had any idea how the woman had known her name, so she hadn't answered. Instead, she had run home.

Several days later, while looking through a family album, chills had run up her spine when she saw a picture of the same woman. She had rushed to her parents with the album, pointing to the picture and blurting, "I saw this lady in the park!"

"That can't be," her mother had said. "That's my Grandma, and she's been dead for twenty years."

"Yeah...couldn't be her...," Anny had said, laughing so her parents would not schedule another trip to the doctor. She knew very well what she had seen. *Was it a ghost?* she wondered. She shuddered, not sure she wanted this to be true.

Mrs. Roanhorse's voice disrupted her thoughts. The woman was waving her hands in the air and saying something very loudly in Navajo to Scout, who was about to run a brush through her hair.

"Mother…," said Jim in exasperation.

"She said not to comb your hair at night because evil spirits will bother you," said Ben, "and to put your hair up before you sleep because ghosts sleep with theirs down."

Scout quickly stuffed the brush into her backpack. "I'm sorry. I didn't know."

"Enough," Jim told his parents. "These poor kids'll be so scared they'll be awake all night."

Outside in the cool night air, he said, "I respect my parents because they are my parents, and in my culture, age brings wisdom, but ignore those old superstitions. I assure you there aren't any ghosts or evil spirits around here—or anywhere else."

"Too bad." Ben poked Scout in the arm. "I wonder if the Girl Scouts have a Ghostbuster badge?"

"Very funny," Scout grumbled, heading for the car.

Anny followed her, then gazed upward at the bright points of light in the dark night sky. "I've never seen so many stars." At home in California, the sky most nights appeared to be a solid gray-black, the stars blocked out by the city lights. Only the brightest showed up. Here, however, the sky was a field of millions of brilliant white dots.

"See that place where the stars look cloudy?" Anny pointed up to a long, hazy pathway that streaked across the starry blackness. "That's the Milky Way."

Scout reached inside the car, pulled out a sleeping bag, and handed it to Anny. "I know. I saw it through the telescope when my Girl Scout troop went to the observatory."

Gazing at the stars, Anny felt very alone, despite the fact she wasn't. She knew how the pioneers must have felt during their long crossings in covered wagons.

"Remember what my grandmother said about looking around too much," teased Ben.

Jim tousled his nephew's hair. "Now don't you start!"

Eric and Jim headed for the car to get their gear.

"We forgot our backpacks inside," Scout told Anny, putting her sleeping bag on the ground. "I'll get them."

As Ben rummaged in the car, Anny looked for a place to put her sleeping bag and shook it out to get it to lie flat.

"Hey, better not do that," warned Ben. "It'll make the ghosties come."

"Your uncle said to stop that."

"And better make sure it doesn't point north. You'll die!" Laughing, he pulled his sleeping bag from the car and carefully unrolled it on the ground.

Anny felt her heart pounding. *I'm not afraid*, she told herself. *Jim is right. These are just old superstitions. I shouldn't believe them.* All the same, she knew the hogan door pointed east, and she made sure her sleeping bag pointed in that direction, just in case.

She heard a horse whinney and looked off toward the corral. Out of the corner of her eye, she saw a movement in the distance. In the bright moonlight, she could make out the silhouette of a rider on a horse, facing her.

Anny ran to the car. "Jim! There's someone out there."

Jim turned around. "At this time of night? Where?"

"On that horse over there!" Anny pointed, but to her shocked amazement, the rider was gone. "He was right out there a few seconds ago! Honest!"

"I wouldn't worry about it," Jim said. "Probably just a neighbor out rounding up sheep. Pretty late for that, though."

As Scout emerged from the hogan with the backpacks, Anny wondered where the rider could have gone so quickly. *There has to be a logical explanation.*

Scout laid her sleeping bag next to Anny's, then pulled a scrunchie from her pack and put her hair up in a ponytail.

Anny shivered in the chilly air. "Are you scared?"

"Who, me? Of course not. I'm just more comfortable with my hair up."

"I'm not scared, either," Anny replied, though she was relieved that her hair was already in a ponytail. She crawled into her sleeping bag and pulled the top up to her chin.

Why isn't Scout lecturing me all about camping and everything she learned about it in Girl Scouts? Her sister *was* scared, whether she wanted to admit it or not. Anny realized that Mrs. Roanhorse's words had frightened her, too, and more than just a little. She shut her eyes tightly, trying to make sure that she didn't look around anymore at the night sky.

Jim and the boys crawled into their sleeping bags. Scout was already in hers.

"Good night, kids," said Jim.

After a long time, Anny heard them breathing deeply, and finally she began to drift off herself.

A whinney brought her back to consciousness. She heard it again, and her heart began to pound. She shut her eyes. *I'm dreaming. I didn't hear a thing.* Then she heard it a third time. *It's a horse in the corral*, she told herself, though she knew the sound came from too far away for that. When the horse whinnied yet again, she knew the sound was real. She swallowed, wondering why no one else had awakened. They were still breathing deeply.

The horse snorted. Anny gathered the courage to open her eyes. Slowly, she sat up. She shivered and wrapped her arms around herself to keep warm.

Silhouetted in the moonlight was the same horse and rider, but much closer this time. The man sat bareback on a dark horse with a white streak down its face. Despite the chilly temperature, he didn't have a shirt on, and his legs were bare, too. He was wearing what she knew was called a breechcloth, and she thought she saw a bow and a quiver of arrows slung over his shoulder.

The rider beckoned her to follow him.

Anny gasped. Quickly, she reached over to shake Scout. "Wake up! Wake up!" she whispered loudly.

"Wha-a-a-?" Scout mumbled.

"He's back! That rider's back!"

"Mm-hm...." Scout rolled over in her sleeping bag.

Anny looked back toward the rider and gasped again when there was no one in sight. A real person wouldn't—couldn't—disappear like that. Mrs. Roanhorse was right! They had looked around too much outside. Scout had brushed her hair. Anny had shaken out her sleeping bag. They both had done all the things it took to call a ghost. She slid into her bedroll, pulled the top over her head, and vowed not to come out until it was broad daylight.

Chapter 7

Anny's hands gripped the top of her sleeping bag. She moved it down over her face, slowly opened her eyes, and squinted as bright sunlight greeted her. Unzipping the bag, she sat up. Scout was still asleep. Birds chirped in the nearby trees, and several sheep milled near the hogan.

A horse snorted, startling her, and she remembered the mysterious rider from the night before. She sat up, looking around for any sign of the stranger. He wasn't there. *Should I tell Jim about him?* she wondered. *He'll just say I was dreaming. Besides, I can't tell him I thought the man was a ghost.*

Just as with her Great-grandma Bradford, she knew what she had seen. She had been wide-awake. Everyone would be sleeping outside again tonight. She had to warn them, so she decided to tell Eric.

Scout rolled over, opened her eyes, and stretched her arms above her head. "I'm hungry."

Good. She doesn't remember anything. Anny glanced at the other sleeping bags. They were empty. "I guess we'll wear the same clothes all day today, too, huh?"

"Just change in your sleeping bag."

Anny felt silly wriggling around in the bag to put on clean underwear, her jeans, and her much-loved red sweatshirt, but she was glad to be in clean clothes.

They rolled up their sleeping bags and put them back in the station wagon. Scout's troop leader would be proud of her, Anny thought, looking at her sister, who was dressed in blue Girl Scout pants—her favorites—and a gray sweatshirt with a big GS on the front.

Scout gazed off at the hogan. "Now what?"

Anny shrugged. "I don't know."

A few minutes later, the door to the hogan opened and Mr. and Mrs. Roanhorse emerged. Jim followed.

"Good morning, girls," he said, as his parents moved away from the hogan and held up their arms to the sky.

"What are they doing?" Scout asked.

"Traditional Navajos pray to Mother Earth and Father Sun every morning." He paused. "Did you sleep well?"

"Terrific!"

"Fine," Anny lied, as guilt stabbed at her again.

"The boys are inside. By the way, I brought some eggs along. I thought you might want some."

"Great!" said Scout.

She sounded relieved, and Anny knew her sister was thinking the same thing she was: Fry bread and corn were delicious, but she didn't want it three meals in a row. Then she realized she wasn't at all hungry. Still shaken from her encounter with the mysterious rider, she didn't think she would be hungry for quite a long time.

46

Not wanting to appear rude, she forced herself to eat the scrambled eggs and toast that Jim cooked on the old stove. Then signing, she asked Eric to come outside. *"I have to tell you what happened last night. I just hope you're not going to think I'm crazy."*

Eric smiled. She could tell he was trying not to laugh at her attempts to use the facial expressions that were as much a part of using sign language as the hand movements themselves, but she knew he was laughing with her, not at her. He often said he was grateful she had learned his language, but she had what the deaf called "foreigner speak." She was usually concentrating so hard on the hand gestures that her face just couldn't keep up. It was like having an accent. Anny thought learning this language was a little like trying to rub her stomach and pat her head at the same time.

When she finished relating the entire story, Eric seemed puzzled. *"Maybe it was just a neighbor, like Jim said."*

"I got a good look at him. He wasn't dressed like any of the Navajos we've seen. More like a warrior from the movies, with a bow and arrows and no clothes except for a—" She didn't know the sign for breechcloth, so she spelled the word letter by letter.

"Maybe it was just one of Ben's practical jokes."

"But the man wanted me to go with him."

"Should we tell Jim?"

"No! Like all adults, he'll say it's all in my head."

"There's one way to prove it isn't—hoofprints. We'll find them. Then we'll have proof to show him."

"You're right! The man was over by the corral the second time and by that big rock the first time. Let's check both places." Anny's hands paused. *"Mr. Roanhorse has horses everywhere. How can we tell the difference between those hoofprints and the ones of the warrior's horse?"*

"I saw it in a movie once. The posse could tell old hoof-prints from new ones because they looked different. We can ask Ben if he knows how to tell them apart. We don't have to say why we want to know."

"Good idea." Anny checked with Ben.

"My grandpa said the old ones don't have sharp edges anymore," he explained, "because sand and leaves and stuff have blown all over them. The new ones have sharp edges." He showed them fresh prints in the corral compared to some old prints outside of it.

A short time later, Anny asked Jim if she and Eric could go for a walk.

"I suppose so. The snakes are still hibernating, but watch out anyway. And be sure to stay within sight of the hogan. Everything looks the same around here, especially to people who aren't familiar with the territory. It's very easy to get lost."

"We will," Anny promised. Taking her camera from her backpack, she slipped it into her pocket.

They first looked at the area where the rider had appeared the second time. To Anny's surprise, there were no hoofprints. *"I know I have the right spot. I don't get it. There should be something."*

"Let's check the other place."

A few minutes later, they reached the location near the big rock where Anny had first seen the rider. She looked around at the sandy desert floor. She saw scrub brush and small plants, but no signs of any hoofprints, new or old. "I know he was right here!" she cried aloud in frustration as she signed the words.

"Maybe he covered up the hoofprints on purpose. He might have missed some. Let's look around some more."

Anny decided to look by the big rock. No prints anywhere. The rock towered over her. She guessed it to be around twenty feet tall. Running her hands over its smooth surface, she studied the large, sandy-colored stone. She walked around to the back; just more sandy-colored rock. A spatter of color caught her eye. "Look!" She grabbed Eric's arm, then pointed to a place on the rock overhead.

Above them was a pictograph like that on the Magic Rock, but this one had no yellow sun. There, in faded, dark-brown paint, was a picture of a galloping horse, and on its back a rider, a man in a breechcloth with flowing black hair and a bow and a quiver of arrows slung across his back.

"That's him!" Anny's hands shook as she signed. *"That's the rider I saw last night!"*

Chapter 8

"Impossible. It's just a painting on a rock."

"That's the man!"

"Well, you can't tell Jim that. He'll think you're crazy."

"Thanks." Although Eric couldn't hear her angry tone, Anny knew he could see her expression. He was the one person she thought she could trust.

"I believe you saw him," he signed quickly. *"Honest I do. We just need more evidence, that's all."*

"We don't have any."

"Then we'll have to wait until he comes back."

"Comes back?" Anny hadn't thought of that.

"You've already seen him twice, so you might see him again. Do you have your camera?"

She nodded. Taking it out, she snapped the rock painting.

"Take a picture of *him* next time. Then you'll have proof."

"Okay.... It can't do any harm to have the camera with me—can it? What if he's a traditional Navajo who doesn't want his image on film? I'll have to be very careful." Her spirits lifted a little as they headed back to the hogan.

When they reached the corral, Mr. Roanhorse, Jim, Scout, and Ben were at the gate.

"We're about to start your riding lessons," Jim said.

"Great!" Eric replied.

"Yeah, great," said Anny, though her thoughts were really on the mysterious warrior.

"I get that horse with the big, white blaze down his face," Scout exclaimed. "You can choose one, too."

"That's cool," Anny told her sister, but she had barely heard Scout's words. She tried to distract herself from the warrior by carefully listening to Jim and Mr. Roanhorse as they explained how to brush a horse and saddle it.

Anny selected a palomino named Nugget. During the hours that they rode, she got the courage to trot the mare a little. Jim and Ben showed her how to sit the saddle so she wouldn't bounce. No matter how hard she tried to concentrate, though, the warrior remained firmly in her thoughts.

That evening, Anny got the nerve to mention the pictograph to Jim. "It looked just like the rider I saw last night."

"Those are all over this area," he said. "They're very interesting, aren't they?"

Jim doesn't hear what I'm saying. How can I convince anyone when I'm the only one who sees the warrior?

As she and Scout got their gear out of the station wagon, Anny mustered her courage to ask Jim another question. "Okay if I sleep inside tonight?"

Jim's eyebrows shot up. "You don't want to sleep outside with your sister?"

"Yeah! You don't want to sleep outside?" echoed Scout.

Anny shook her head. "I guess I'm not much of a camper." She hated fibbing, but she couldn't tell Jim or anyone else the truth. Not yet. She couldn't risk another accusation of an overactive imagination.

"I don't think my parents will mind," Jim said.

"I'll sleep inside, too, if you want," Scout offered.

"That's okay. I know you'd rather be outside."

As Scout started arranging her sleeping bag, Anny took Eric aside. *"I'll be in the hogan. If you see a horse and rider tonight, tell Jim right away."*

"I will."

Anny lay awake for a long time before falling into a restless sleep. When she awoke, rays of sunshine poured through the windows, creating squares of light on the dirt floor. Mrs. Roanhorse and Jim busied themselves around the stove. Instantly, Anny thought of Eric and wondered if he had seen the warrior.

"Good morning," said Jim.

"Good morning," she answered. Jumping up, she rushed past him and out the door to find the two boys and Scout still fast asleep.

She knelt down beside Eric and began to shake him.

He slowly opened his eyes. "Mm-mm...?"

"Did you see him?" she signed.

"Who?"

"The warrior!"

Eric sat up. *"No. I've been asleep all night."*

Anny rested on her heels and sighed heavily.

"Don't worry. We'll get that picture soon."

She knew he was trying to make her feel better, but it wasn't working. *Why am I the only one who sees strange people and things?*

"Time for breakfast!" Jim called from the doorway.

Anny forced herself to eat, but she still felt disappointed.

"How about going out to see Dr. Sanderson's dig?" Jim suggested.

At that, she perked up. "Yeah!" she said, along with the others.

After they packed the car, they all thanked Mr. and Mrs. Roanhorse for showing them a great time.

"Come back again soon," Mr. Roanhorse said, but he was looking straight at Anny.

As she gazed back at the man, she got the feeling that he had something to tell her. Frustrated that whatever it was would have to wait, she hoped they would get the chance to visit the hogan again before they had to go home.

Jim pulled the station wagon off the highway then drove almost thirty minutes across the sandy desert. Rounding a large rock outcropping, Anny spotted Dr. Sanderson and Bill, in jeans and sweatshirts, standing by an area surrounded by stakes. Behind them were several large, wooden crates. Propped against the sides were the crate lids, several shovels, and some pick-axes. Dr. Sanderson pushed his hat back on his head and watched as they drove up.

Jim stopped the car and turned off the motor.

"This is so cool!" said Scout.

"Archaeological digs are scientific places," Jim said. "Be sure to go only where Dr. Sanderson says it's okay."

"We will." Scout flung open the door and rushed out.

"Hello!" Jim called to the two men.

"Hello...," Dr. Sanderson answered, but from his tone, Anny could tell he wasn't very happy to see them.

She quickly slipped her camera into her pocket. *This is what Scout means by being prepared. Maybe I can write about the dig for the school newspaper.* Zipping her jacket against the chill, she followed the others over to where the two men were standing. White string hung from one stake to the next around the edge of the pit, as Dr. Sanderson called it, which was about two feet deep and ten feet across.

Jim scratched his chin. "I've seen digs before," he said. "I thought the stakes and string were supposed to go across the pit, too—in a grid pattern. At least that's the way all the other digs I've seen have been strung out."

Dr. Sanderson's gaze darted at Bill and back to Jim. "Uh...we haven't gotten that far yet...."

Jim's eyebrows rose. "But you've already started digging. What are you hoping to find?"

"Pottery, stone tools, things like that." The archaeologist began rifling through one of the crates, removing some more shovels and other tools. "We have a long way to go first."

"How far down are you going to dig?" asked Scout.

"About eight or ten feet." Dr. Sanderson dropped a shovel into the middle of the pit.

Bill explained what they were doing as the archaeologist continued unpacking the crate.

Anny noticed a large group of boulders about thirty feet away and thought she saw a narrow path between them. Curious, she decided to investigate. As she neared the base, she paused to study the path, shoving her hands into her jacket pockets to keep them warm.

"I wouldn't go near those rocks if I were you."

Startled, Anny wheeled around to see Dr. Sanderson standing behind her, staring at her through narrowed eyes. His thin lips formed a hard line, his hands clenched into fists at his sides. Familiar apprehension began creeping over her.

"There are snakes all through there," he warned, "and you sure don't want to get bitten by one."

That's funny. Jim said they were still hibernating.

The archaeologist stood rooted, and Anny knew he wasn't going to move until she did. The fact he didn't want her going behind the rocks told her something was back there. Trying to control her uneasiness, she was determined to find out what.

At the pit, her chance came almost immediately. Dr. Sanderson had been having trouble with his truck again, and he asked Ben to have another look at it. While they were both bent under the hood, Anny slipped back to the rocks.

The path winding upward between the two large boulders seemed well-worn, and she didn't see any snakes as she followed it to an open area between two even larger rocks. She stopped short as the sun glinted off of metal. *Are these what Dr. Sanderson didn't want me to see?*

Chapter 9

Lying on their sides in the clearing were several gas cans. The caps were off and she smelled the telltale odor of gasoline. Reaching for the handle on a can, she lifted it up.

Flames flashed before her, and she gasped for air as a vision of fire once again threatened her. Dropping the can, she stumbled backward, tripped, and fell to the ground. She propped herself up on her elbows and took a deep breath. The vision stopped as suddenly as it had started. Sitting up, she clutched her chest, trying to calm her rapidly beating heart.

The gas can was empty. She wanted to tap the others with her shoe but didn't for fear that the vision would return. From their missing caps, though, she knew they were empty.

Why wouldn't Dr. Sanderson want me to see these gas cans? Why would picking one up make me have another vision? Then her breath caught in her throat. *Did Dr. Sanderson and Bill start the fire at the school?* She had to tell Jim!

Jogging back down the path, she stopped and peered around a boulder to make sure the archaeologists were still busy with Ben under the hood of their truck. Jim was leaning under the hood, too. Scout stood beside him.

Anny quietly approached the group without notice.

"We'll need a wrench for this job," Jim said. "I'll get one."

She followed him back to the station wagon. When they were out of earshot, the words spilled out. "Dr. Sanderson didn't want me to go behind those rocks. He said rattlesnakes were there, but you said they're still hibernating. I saw a bunch of empty gas cans back there." She paused to catch her breath. "I think he and Bill set the fire at the school!"

"Now don't jump to conclusions." Jim opened the tailgate and retrieved a wrench. "It's common for people here to have gas cans handy. There isn't a station anywhere for miles." Shutting the tailgate, he returned to the truck.

He's like all the others. He doesn't believe me! Anny stood in shocked disappointment, angry she had set herself up once again. She had felt like this so many times she had lost count. She hated it. *How can I tell him about my visions without him thinking I'm crazy?*

Something made her look up. She gasped. The mysterious warrior stood on his horse atop the boulders she had just walked between. She could see his face clearly. He was about the same age as her youngest uncle, who was twenty-five. His dark eyes bored straight down at her, his black hair flowing down his shoulders, his skin bronze and shiny. His hands rested on the horse's neck and held rope reins.

It's broad daylight. I'm not dreaming now! Anny spun around, ready to shout his presence to everyone, but Dr. Sanderson was facing the warrior. He obviously saw no one but Jim standing in front of him.

A photo! Looking back at the warrior and without taking her eyes off of him, she yanked her camera from her pocket and raised it to her eyes. She blinked. She couldn't find the man in the viewfinder. Pulling the camera away from her face, she stared straight at him, then raised it to her eyes at exactly that place. Still no one showed up. Her heart began to pound again as she realized that he wasn't visible in the lens.

Without moving her gaze from the warrior, she put away the camera, then stepped sideways over to the truck and grabbed Eric's arm. *"The warrior is on top of those rocks over there,"* she signed.

Eric looked over at the boulders as Jim and Dr. Sanderson leaned under the hood again. Then he pulled Anny away from the truck. *"I don't see anything."*

"He's right on top of that rock!"

Eric's face drained of color. *"Maybe he is a ghost."*

Shivers ran up Anny's spine as her hands signed furiously. *"He can't be! Can't you see through ghosts? This man is a solid person!"*

"Did you take a picture?"

"I tried, but he doesn't show up in the viewfinder."

"Then he's a ghost. Take a picture anyway. I read they show up when you get the film developed. For some reason, you're the only one who can see him."

"Then you believe me?" Anny held her breath.

"Yes, I do."

"Scout and I broke some of those rules Mrs. Roanhorse warned us about at the hogan. That must be why he's here."

Anny could hardly believe that the mysterious rider was a ghost, but if he wasn't, his horse would have left hoofprints. She had never heard of a horse being a ghost, though. Maybe the man was just good at covering his tracks, as Eric had said earlier. *But if he* is *a ghost, is he good or evil?*

The warrior beckoned to her, just as he had done at the hogan, and once again, shivers ran up her spine. Then the man turned his horse and disappeared down the other side of the boulders.

"He's going away! I have to follow him this time!"

"No!" Eric cried.

Ignoring him, she glanced back at the others, who were still engrossed under the truck's hood. Her heart pounded and her hands were clammy as she raced back to the rocks. Eric's footsteps thundered behind her. She ran up the path and into the clearing again. How she got there without anyone hearing or noticing, she didn't understand. *Did something stop them from seeing me? Has the warrior cast a spell on them?*

She reached the clearing, but the rider was gone. *"Where did he go?"*

"I don't know, but ghosts can go anywhere." Eric pointed to the gas cans. *"What are those for?"*

"I found them earlier. I know it sounds crazy, but when I picked one of them up, I had another vision of the fire. I think it means Dr. Sanderson and Bill started the fire at the school."

"What?"

"Yeah. I told Jim, but he didn't believe me. He said Dr. Sanderson probably needed extra gas for his truck."

"Then why wouldn't he put them where they would be handy to his truck instead of carting them way up here?" Eric picked up one of the cans, studied it, then set it back on the ground. *"You may be right. Dr. Sanderson had something to do with that fire. Quick! Take a picture!"*

Anny pulled out her camera and lined up the gas cans in the viewfinder. They showed up perfectly. She snapped the shutter, sure now that her camera was working.

"We have to find more proof."

Returning the camera to her pocket, she let out a long breath. *"Right now I want to find that warrior."* She peered around a boulder to discover another path leading down the back side of the rocks. *"Maybe he's down here."* She started along the path with Eric behind her once again.

They were soon back in the wide expanse of desert with no sign of the warrior. Anny could feel beads of sweat rolling down her face and the hairs on the back of her neck standing on end. She gulped. Solid form or no solid form, the man *had* to be a ghost. No *real* person could disappear from sight on the open desert that fast. From the look on Eric's stark-white face, she realized he shared her thoughts.

They looked at each other a moment, then Eric signed, *"I wonder what he wants?"*

"I don't know...." Anny stared at the sweeping space. *"We'd better get back before we get in trouble."*

They turned to go up the path, but Anny stopped in her tracks.

Eric bumped into her. *"What's wrong?"*

"Look...!" She pointed to the boulder in front of them.

There, just above their heads, was another pictograph, a very faded picture of a large rock with an arched top and a gaping hole in the middle of it.

"That looks like Window Rock," said Eric.

"This is the second rock painting we've found right where I saw the warrior. That can't just be coincidence." Anny reached-ed up to touch it. *"It's faded like the other one, so it must be old. Is this what he wanted me to see? I just don't understand what any of this could possibly mean."*

"This is the third rock painting we've seen since we got here. Remember the picture of the sun and the horses on the Magic Rock at the school?"

Anny was taken aback. *"Do you think that has anything to do with this?"*

"Well, Dr. Sanderson was at the school when we found the Magic Rock. You and the ghost were at the rock painting by the hogan. Now you, it, the ghost, and Dr. Sanderson are all here at this dig. There must be a connection. Maybe the ghost is trying to tell you something."

"But what?" Before Eric could answer, Anny quickly snapped a photo of the pictograph. She had to get back to Jim's house and her laptop so she could check for Aunt Elaine's e-mail message about what Dr. Sanderson was doing here. She also wanted to check for information about the treasure. Some-how, she knew the answers were there.

Chapter 10

Only when Anny and Eric were once again standing beside the old blue pickup did anyone seem to notice them. Anny looked at Eric, and from the expression on his face, she knew he agreed with what she was thinking. The warrior must have cast a spell on them.

Once Jim and Ben got the truck running, they all piled into the car for the ride back to Jim's house. Anny could hardly wait to check her e-mail messages.

The drive seemed endless, but finally, Jim pulled into his driveway. Anny bounded from the car and waited impatiently while Jim unlocked the front door.

Inside, she grabbed her laptop, then paused to look at the painting of Window Rock over the couch. Convinced now that the pictograph was of that same formation, she turned to Jim. "Okay if I get on the Internet?"

"Yes. I'm not expecting any calls at the moment."

Anny touched Eric's arm, then nodded toward the kitchen table. Eric followed her.

She quickly plugged in the computer, then sat down and got online, praying an e-mail from Ben's aunt would be there.

When she saw a message with the extension "ua.edu," she pointed to it, then signed, *"That has to be from Ben's Aunt Elaine!"* She clicked on it, her gaze flying over the words:

Hi, Ben,

Good to hear from you. Glad you're having a good time visiting Uncle Jim. I don't know Dr. Sanderson personally, but according to his secretary, he was very excited about picking up his new, white SUV and driving it to Navajo Land to work on a dig. The only other thing I can add is that he's very popular with his students and he's done a lot of very important archaeological work. Sorry I don't have any more information.

Love,

Aunt Elaine

"New, white SUV?" Eric signed.

"What happened to it?" Anny thought about the old pickup and all of its mechanical problems. *"Dr. Sanderson didn't even mention having a new car. In fact, I remember him saying he knew he'd have to buy a new one soon."*

"Should we tell Jim?"

Anny wasn't so sure, but she nodded. They showed the message to everyone. "If he bought a new car, why didn't he say so? And where is it?"

"He probably didn't want to drive it out here," said Jim. "Cars can get very dusty in the desert."

Anny almost opened her mouth to protest. There was no convincing Jim. She and Eric were on their own in proving Dr. Sanderson's guilt. Instead, she said, "Where was he going in Navajo Land?"

63

"Good question," said Ben. "It covers part of Northern Arizona and New Mexico and Southern Colorado and Utah."

"Maybe we can drive over to Four Corners, where you can stand in the four states at one time," added Jim.

"I'd love a photo of that!" Sitting at the computer, Anny typed "lost treasure of the golden sun" into the browser's search field. A moment later, a list popped up, and she studied it carefully. Lost Dutchman's Mine—*that was the one Jim had mentioned*—Lost Treasure of the Knights Templar, Lost Treasure of the Ark, Lost Treasure of the Ghaznavids—she could hardly pronounce that one—Lost Treasure Book Sales, Lost Treasure Finders Newsletter—Lost Treasure of the Golden Sun.

She gasped and grabbed Eric's arm. There it was! Lost Treasure of the Golden Sun. She clicked the link. A few seconds later, a new screen appeared. She scanned the words. The article repeated the story of the lost treasure almost the way Mr. Roanhorse had told it to them. Diego Garza had hidden the treasure to keep it from the *conquistadores* who were chasing him. There was more at the bottom:

In the pocket of the man found wandering in the desert was this poem:

Look for the snowy peak so tall
behind the open portal wall.
When the sun shines o'er the circle round,
lines you'll draw, then you'll have found,
the warrior at his secret lair.
Get past his arrows if you dare.
Fifty paces down you'll walk
to see the sun upon the rock.
Then dig beneath that golden sun,
and Spanish treasure you'll have won.

Archaeologists claim that whoever solves the riddle of this poem will find the treasure, if it is still buried in its original location.

Diego Garza's descendents have offered a reward of $100,000 for the return of the family's golden cross, supposedly buried with this treasure.

Anny saved the article to her hard drive. *"Look for the snowy peak so tall behind the open portal wall...."* She pointed to the painting over the couch. *"I'll bet the open portal is Window Rock and the snowy peak is a mountain behind it."*

Eric looked at the artwork. *"Yeah!"*

When the sun shines o'er the circle round, a line you'll draw, then you'll have found..., Anny read silently. *Wouldn't the sun shine directly over the rock formation at noon? That line seems kind of weird.* She continued reading. The warrior at the secret lair....

The warrior! She grabbed Eric's arm again. Pointing to the words, she stared at him; he stared right back at her. Was the warrior she had seen the same one referred to in this poem?

She rushed to her sister's side. "Got a pen and paper?" She heard her own frantic tone.

"Sure." Scout fished through her backpack and retrieved a small pad of paper and a pen. "What's so important?"

Anny snatched the pad and pen from her sister and rushed back to the table. "Tell you in a minute."

She scribbled down the poem, then stood up. *Do I dare tell everyone about this?* Knowing she was risking ridicule, she gathered her courage and announced, "I have something to read to you all."

When she was sure she had their attention, she read slowly so they heard every word. After she finished, she looked at them. "This tells us just where to find the treasure!"

Scout and Ben rushed to look at the poem in her hand.

"It seems to be about the treasure, all right," said Scout, "but how do we know it's for real?"

"She's right," Ben agreed.

"It says the treasure is beneath the golden sun. See?" Anny insisted. "Remember? Dr. Sanderson thought the treasure was beneath the golden sun." She recited the line from the poem. "Then dig beneath that golden sun and Spanish treasure you'll have won. The Magic Rock has a golden sun on it." She paused, wondering if she should let them in on her suspicions, then summoned her courage once again. "I think that Dr. Sanderson was digging for the treasure at the school. I think he's the one who burned it down."

Jim put his arms up. "Whoa! I know it would be fun to find a buried treasure, but don't let your imagination run away with you. You can't accuse someone without proof. Scout and Ben are right. That poem can't mean anything."

"Why?" Anny was upset that Jim still didn't believe her.

"Because if Diego Garza had written it, he would have done so in Spanish. It would have rhymed in Spanish. Even if it didn't, it certainly wouldn't rhyme when translated into English, unless someone was very clever. That poem does rhyme, so it probably was written by an English speaker. Sorry to disappoint you all, but it's no doubt a fake. It won't lead you to any treasure."

Anny's arms dropped to her sides. She was angry with herself. Of course Jim was right about the rhyming. Diego Garza couldn't have written this poem. *Once again, I've set myself up.*

Scout pulled her off to the side of the room. "You've got to stop this," she whispered. "You're going to get us sent home. And you're embarrassing me!"

Her sister's words stung, and Anny fought back tears. The look in Scout's eyes was stern. Anny had seen it so many times on Mom's face. She could handle most people's hostility toward her, even Mom's, but not Scout's. For all her wishing that she and Scout would be as close as they had been in the past, it seemed instead that they were growing further and further apart.

"I know I'm right!" she wanted to shout, but she kept silent, wondering if she were wrong. *Am I crazy?* She almost admitted defeat, but then she felt a ray of hope. What if Dr. Sanderson had found the poem, too? Maybe he didn't realize it might not be real. Maybe he believed it was true and that the treasure was still here. She thought about her vision of the fire, confused by the jumble of clues. *The truth is there someplace, and I have to work hard to straighten them all out.*

And what about the warrior? She *had* seen him. Mr. Roanhorse had said a warrior guarded the treasure *and* that he had cast an evil spell on the man who tried to find it. The warrior might have cast a spell on everyone at the dig so that she and Eric could find the gas cans and the rock painting. Jim may be right about the rhyming, but he wasn't right about the poem's being a fake. There *was* a warrior and she had seen him. Anny tore off the top sheet of the pad, then fighting back tears, handed the pad and pen back to her sister. This poem held truth, and if she and Eric were going to prove it and Dr. Sanderson's guilt, they would have to do it alone. She looked forward to another encounter with the mysterious phantom.

Chapter 11

Anny sat back down at the computer and logged off the Internet, wondering how she and Eric could possibly solve the mystery without the help of Jim and the others. No sooner had she disconnected the computer when the phone rang, disrupting her thoughts.

Jim picked up the receiver. "Hello? Oh, hello, Mrs. Nakai." He paused a moment. "I think so. We'll see you then. Goodbye." He hung up. "Mrs. Nakai wants us to meet her tomorrow morning in the school cafeteria. It's still in good shape. She'd like to discuss the science fair."

"Great!" said Ben.

Anny's thoughts were far removed from the science fair now. She wanted to go back into the desert to find the warrior. And what had Mr. Roanhorse wanted to tell her? She suspected it had something to do with the treasure, but she would have no way of knowing until she could see the man again. *Is he right that spirits are evil?*

On the drive to the school the next morning, Anny tried to remember her ideas for the fair and to listen as Ben, Eric, and

Scout discussed theirs. It was difficult. Her mind was on other things.

Soon they were again bouncing over the dusty road to the school. Only one car, a beige one, was in front of the building this time. Jim parked outside the school's gates.

As they entered the courtyard, Mrs. Nakai emerged from a set of double doors off to the side. "Hello, everyone!" she called. "Come in."

Anny glanced at the burned classrooms at the back of the courtyard as they followed the principal. Her frustration grew. *How am I ever going to prove Dr. Sanderson is responsible for this? Would Mrs. Nakai ever believe it?*

The principal led them into an open room with several rows of long tables and benches and asked them to sit at one, on which she had placed pads of paper and pencils. "We can brainstorm and write some ideas first, then pick the ones we like."

"Sounds good to me," said Jim. "Kids?"

"Sounds good," the others agreed.

Anny found herself totally focused on the discussion and eagerly writing down ideas, then offering her suggestions for organizing the science fair. As her sister and Eric were adding their comments, she felt a strong desire to turn around and look out the window. She did so—and gasped. In the courtyard, not fifteen feet away, the warrior sat on his dark horse. He gazed at her, the feathers hanging from his long, black hair ruffling slightly in the breeze. Multi-colored beads decorated the tops of his moccasins. Feathers on the ends of the arrows peeked out over his shoulder from the quiver slung across his back. Her heart began to pound as she realized the warrior had made her turn to look at him!

Anny glanced at Mrs. Nakai and Jim. Both of them were facing the courtyard as they continued their discussion, and it was very obvious that neither of them saw anything. *This is just like when we were at the dig.* Anny looked at the warrior.

He lifted his arm and beckoned to her, just as he had done twice before. Then he laid the reins across his horse's neck, turned the animal, rode over to one of the burned classrooms, and pointed to the ground.

I'll be right there, Anny found herself thinking to him, wondering how she could ever get outside. She had an idea, but she had to go alone. Then she stopped herself. *What if the warrior is evil?* She shouldn't be paying any attention to him. Something pulled at her, though, and she knew she had to take the risk. She raised her hand.

"Do you have another idea?" Mrs. Nakai asked.

"Could I please go to the bathroom?"

"Of course." Mrs. Nakai pointed to another set of doors. "Through there and turn left. It's a few doors down."

"I have to go, too," said Scout.

Oh, no! Anny thought. *How am I going to get outside now?* She didn't want anyone to know what she was doing but realized she had no choice but to take her sister with her.

Anny headed for the doors with Scout right behind her. Out in the hall, she said, "Go ahead. I have something to do first. I'll meet you in the bathroom." She ran for the doors to the courtyard.

"What?" Scout answered, trying to keep up. "You said you had to go to the bathroom. Why are you going outside?"

Anny hoped the warrior would keep her and her sister hidden from everyone's view as she investigated where he wanted her to look. When she rushed outside, the warrior was gone. She looked around in disappointment. *He wanted me to come out here. Why would he disappear now?*

Scout stood hands on hips. "Annwyn Brady, do you mind telling me what we're doing out here?"

Anny gave her sister a dirty look. Scout knew how much she disliked her real name. Nobody else in the world was called Annwyn, but for some reason he had never explained, her grandfather had insisted she have it. *A weird name for an even weirder girl*, she thought, wondering for the millionth time why she couldn't have been given a more normal-sounding one like her sister's. *And why can't I be normal, too?*

Without a word, she went to the place beside the burned building where the warrior had pointed. When she reached it, she stared in disbelief. "Look!"

"What?" Scout ambled over to Anny, clearly annoyed.

Anny pointed to the ground. "Two more holes! I know those weren't here the other day!"

"You're right...." Scout's expression changed from quizzical to confident. "Maybe the fire fighters or police did that."

"Come on, think about it. Why would firefighters or police dig under the building?" Anny peered closer into one of the holes. "I see something down there." Then she lay down at the edge.

"Be careful! You might fall in."

"Hold my legs!" Anny leaned farther over the edge. When she felt her sister grip her ankles firmly, she scooted forward as far as she could and stretched out her hand. *Just a little more and I can reach it*, she thought.

"You're going to fall in!" Scout warned again, "and we're going to get caught!"

"Just hang on to me!" Anny inched over the edge a little more, and her fingertips brushed the object. She almost had it! Stretching as far as she could, she wrapped her fingertips around it, then yanked hard. "Got it!"

Chapter 12

"Now pull me up!" On her feet, Anny turned the object over, then stumbled back, dropping it in horror. Vicious, crackling flames appeared in front of her, and she reeled backwards trying to escape them. Coughing as she inhaled black smoke, she waved her hands to avoid choking. This experience was as strong as the one she had had on their first trip to the school.

"What's wrong?" Scout cried.

Anny fought off the vision, telling herself it wasn't real. Gasping for breath, she shut her eyes, sank to her knees, and covered her face with her hands. She felt her sister's arm around her shoulder.

"What's happening? What is it?" Scout asked, alarm still edging her voice.

As suddenly as the noise of the crackling fire was there, it disappeared. Slowly, Anny removed her hands from her face. The entire vision was gone. She took a deep breath, as much to calm herself as to clear her lungs.

"What is it?" Scout asked again. "Are you all right?"

Unable to speak, Anny closed her eyes for a moment, then nodded, pointing to the ground.

There lay a beaded leather headband with a large turquoise stone in the center.

"That looks just like the one on Dr. Sanderson's hat," said Scout.

Anny nodded again, her throat too parched to talk.

Scout paused for a moment, her eyes narrowing. "It's almost as though you knew that was in that hole. How?"

Do I dare tell her the truth? Anny couldn't stand the idea of her sister thinking the worst of her. She decided to risk telling her the whole story anyway. If she had any chance of building a closer relationship with her twin, Scout had to know everything. Anny cleared her throat. "This is going to sound crazy, but I keep having a vision of a fire and lots of smoke."

Scout's eyes remained narrowed. "Is that what happened to you on our first day here?"

Anny nodded. "There's more...." She paused, biting her lip, then took a deep breath and plunged in. "The warrior from the poem has been appearing to me."

"What?" Scout's eyes widened and her mouth fell open. "Jim said that poem isn't even real!"

"It *is* real," Anny insisted. "He's appeared to me four times now. Twice the night we slept at the hogan, again at the dig, and now here. He's sitting on a horse and has long, black hair with feathers in it. He wears moccasins and has a quiver of arrows over his shoulder!"

"You're right. This *is* crazy!"

Anny winced. "In both places I saw him I found pictographs," she went on, desperate for Scout to believe her. "One was of the warrior and the one at the dig was of Window Rock with a snowy peak behind it. I took pictures of both of them."

"The dig? When did you find anything there?"

"While everybody was working on the truck."

"But you were right there with us! You never left!"

"Yes, I did. I think the warrior cast a spell on you so you wouldn't see us leave."

"A spell?" Scout rolled her eyes in total disbelief. Then she paused. "Us? Who's 'us'?"

"Eric went with me. Ask him."

Scout's mouth fell open again, but she didn't speak.

"The warrior was right here in the courtyard, pointing to these holes. He obviously wanted me to find this headband." She nodded toward the cafeteria. "Look." Inside, the principal and Jim were deep in discussion with Eric and Ben. "They're facing the windows and don't even see us. I think the warrior cast a spell on them so we could come out here."

Scout stared at her, then walked slowly toward the windows, waving her arms.

"That won't do any good. They can't see you."

Scout continued walking and waving her arms. Only when she was in front of the windows did she finally stop and look back. "You're right...." Her voice was barely above a whisper. She returned to Anny. "You're telling me you see ghosts?"

Anny nodded. "I think so...."

"And other things that I don't?" Scout went on. "This has happened before, hasn't it? These are what you've been seeing that made Mom take you to those doctors...."

"Yes...." Anny paused. "I'm not crazy. You heard Mr. Roanhorse. He has visions, too." She grasped Scout's arm. "Don't tell anyone, though. Promise! They won't believe me."

Scout let out a long breath. "I promise." Her eyes widened. "Aren't you scared? I mean—*ghosts!*" She cringed. "I sure don't want to see them! What does the warrior want?"

"I didn't know at first, but now I think he's trying to help me prove Dr. Sanderson is looking for the treasure."

"Then if the headband was in this hole, does that mean that Dr. Sanderson dug it—and the other ones...?" Without awaiting an answer, Scout added, "And that he started the fire?"

"I don't know," Anny said, "but it sure looks that way."

"Then you were right all along...." Scout put her arms around Anny and gave her a big hug. "I'm sorry for not believing you before."

Anny basked in that hug. It was a long time coming, and now she felt sure she and Scout could be close again. "I've missed you," she whispered.

"Me, too...." Scout pushed away from Anny. "We have to tell Jim and Mrs. Nakai!"

Anny grabbed her sister's arm. "Wait! Let's not mention the warrior, okay? Let's just tell them about the holes and the headband. That's the truth, anyway." She looked down at the piece of beaded leather. "Can you carry that in? I'm afraid if I touch it again, my vision will come back."

Scout nodded, then blinked. "Do you think I'll have a vision if I pick it up?"

"I don't think so...."

Scout tentatively reached out a hand to tap the headband. "No vision...." She picked it up.

The two went back inside, but not before Anny looked again for the warrior. There was no sign of him. *He'll come when the time is right.*

Back in the cafeteria, Mrs. Nakai looked at them in surprise. "That was fast. You left just seconds ago."

"There are two more holes in the courtyard under one of the burned classrooms," Scout blurted out, "and we found Dr. Sanderson's headband there!" Scout thrust her hand forward, the stone in the center of her palm, the beaded leather band draping down both sides. "See?"

For someone who hadn't believed her suspicions at first, Scout certainly seemed convinced of Dr. Sanderson's guilt now. Anny ignored the quizzical look on Eric's face.

"Courtyard?" asked Mrs. Nakai. "When did you have time to go out there?"

"Just now!" said Scout before Anny could stop her. "You have to go look!"

Jim frowned. "We didn't see you out there."

"You were busy talking to everyone," Anny said. "You probably just didn't notice us. We'll show you."

Outside, everyone peered into the holes.

"Scout's right," said Mrs. Nakai. "These weren't here the other day."

"Maybe the firefighters dug them," said Jim.

"Dr. Sanderson dug them," insisted Anny, "and this headband is the proof!"

Jim took the beaded leather from Scout. "I'll admit it looks like the one Dr. Sanderson has, but these are sold all over the Navajo Nation. My own father has one. You've seen it. We can't accuse anyone on evidence like this."

"But your dad's doesn't have that turquoise stone in the middle," Anny protested, as he handed the headband back to Scout. Jim still didn't believe her! She knew Eric and Scout did. Now she just had to convince Ben. Maybe he could influence his uncle. Then there was Mr. Roanhorse. She had to get to the hogan.

Off in the distance, a phone rang.

"I'll be right back," Mrs. Nakai told them and hurried back into the building.

Eric studied the headband. "It really does look like Dr. Sanderson's."

Mrs. Nakai returned shortly. "That was the FBI," she said to Jim. "They're also investigating the fire. Their agent is driving over today. He wants to talk to us both, and it might take some time."

The science teacher thought a moment. "Well, the kids could go back to my dad's for the afternoon...."

Yes! Anny cried silently. *Was this sudden development the warrior's handiwork, too?* Whether it was or not, she was going to get the chance to talk to Mr. Roanhorse!

Chapter 13

Anny knew she had to convince Mr. Roanhorse to let them go riding and to talk the others into going to the dig. If the archaeologist's headband wasn't on his hat where it belonged, she would have the proof she needed of his guilt. *But first I have to find out if Mr. Roanhorse has something to tell me.*

They didn't have to wait for Ben's grandfather this time. As they stepped from the car, he emerged from the hogan, dressed in a blue shirt and jeans. Sun glinted off his silver belt buckle. "What has happened, my son?"

"Nothing, Dad," Jim assured him. "Just the FBI. The agent wants to talk to Mrs. Nakai and me about the fire. The kids'll have more fun being out here than waiting for me."

Mr. Roanhorse smiled, glancing knowingly at Anny. "Yes. Leave them here."

I was right, she thought in anticipation. *He does have something to tell me.*

"Can we go riding, Mr. Roanhorse?" Scout asked.

"Of course."

Thank you, Scout! Anny cried to herself. Things were working out just perfectly!

"You kids have fun, then," said Jim. "I'll be back this evening to get you."

After Jim left, Ben said, "Let's saddle up!"

He, Scout, and Eric headed off to the corral, but not before Anny asked Scout to give Mr. Roanhorse the headband. Anny lingered back to tell him how she found it and why she couldn't touch it. "I know this is Dr. Sanderson's and I think he's treasure-hunting, but Jim doesn't believe me."

He gently fingered the beaded leather, then said quietly, "An evil spirit inhabits the person who wears this."

"Then you *do* believe there are spirits." Anny was almost afraid to say it.

Mr. Roanhorse looked at her, his black eyes intense. "All of us who follow the Old Ways believe in them." He shook his head. "I am afraid my son does not." He paused a moment, then said, "You have visions, don't you?"

Anny swallowed. "How did you know?"

Mr. Roanhorse sat down on an old wooden box. "A person who has them can recognize another person who does."

"Then you believe they're real."

"Of course they are real. We call ghosts *chindi*. Most of my people are afraid of them. They think they are what we call skinwalkers—you call them witches or evil spirits—and sometimes they are, and then you can get ghost sickness."

"Ghost sickness?"

"Yes. The disease you get when evil spirits follow you. But some visions are signs. They tell us something or show us the path we are to follow. People who see them are special."

"Is that what you wanted to tell me? I mean—I got the feeling you had something to say. Was this it?"

Mr. Roanhorse nodded.

"Nobody has ever believed me," Anny said, as relief swept over her. *I'm finally talking to someone who understands me!* "They say that I'm making things up or that I have an overactive imagination. Some people have even told me I'm crazy. My mom's been taking me to psychiatrists and psychologists to see what's wrong."

Mr. Roanhorse shook his head. "A-a-g-g-hh. *Biligaani.*"

"Biligonny?" she repeated, confused.

"White people. They have lost touch with what is important. They call you crazy, when they should be learning from the things you feel and see. I am just like you, but in my culture, I am considered holy. That is why I am a *hataalii,* a shaman, a medicine man—sort of a combination of what you call a minister, rabbi, or priest and a doctor. I believe what you sense about Dr. Sanderson. The white man's medicine can't help you with this." He fell silent.

Anny summoned her courage. "I've seen the warrior from the legend. Four times now—if you count the first night when I saw him twice."

Mr. Roanhorse's gaze met hers.

She told him about the sightings at the hogan, the dig, and the school, and about finding the pictographs at the first two locations and the headband at the last.

"He was *here?*" The man looked worried. "That is not good at all."

Anny wondered if she and Scout had conjured up the ghost by their behavior, after all. Maybe she *did* have ghost sickness. As Mr. Roanhorse continued studying the beaded leather, she considered asking him if there was a cure, but he spoke before she had the chance.

"What did he look like?"

"His hair is long with feathers in it. He wears a breech-cloth and moccasins, and he doesn't have a shirt on. And he has a bow and a quiver of arrows across his back."

"He is not *Diné*. The *Diné* do not dress like that. We are sheep ranchers, not warriors. I believe he is Anasazi, an Ancient One."

"The people who lived here before your people came?"

Mr. Roanhorse nodded.

Anny pulled the copy of the poem from her pocket and read all of it to him. She pointed to a line. "This says, 'The warrior at the secret lair.' It has to be the same warrior."

He nodded again.

"I think he's trying to help me prove Dr. Sanderson is treasure-hunting and that he set the fire at the school."

"Perhaps, but the *Diné* believe it is not good to be around the dead. When someone dies in a hogan, the family cuts a hole in the back to let the person's spirit out. Then they leave. No one ever lives in that hogan again. It is the only way to avoid ghost sickness. You must be very careful. You must learn the difference between true visions and ghost sickness. This spirit seems to want more."

"How can I tell? He keeps asking me to follow him. I don't want to if he's bad, but he doesn't seem to be."

"You can tell by looking into his eyes, for they are the window to the soul," Mr. Roanhorse answered. "But that is far too dangerous." He stood up and put the headband on the box. "I will keep this safe for you."

Fingering the little pouch that hung from the leather string around his neck, he said, "You must have protection against him in case he is evil. Wait here."

He disappeared into the hogan, then returned a moment later with something in his hand. He removed the pouch from around his neck. Setting down another small leather bag, he opened it up, then opened the one he had taken off and poured some of its contents into his hand. "This is gall medicine," he said, pouring it into the second little bag. "It will protect you."

When he was done, he put the string holding the first pouch back over his head and hung the second one around Anny's neck. "No evil spirit can harm you now."

Anny took a deep breath, then touched the pouch as relief swept over her once again. "I feel better already. Thank you." She knew part of her relief was finally having an adult who believed her, an adult who didn't think she was crazy.

Now she just had to convince Scout, Eric, and Ben to ride with her to the dig.

Chapter 14

Anny strode to the corral. Scout and Eric already believed her. She studied Ben, who wore a cowboy hat low over his eyes as he brushed down his brown mare. Particles of dust rose in little reddish clouds with each stroke of the bristles over the mare's back. Scout and Eric stood beside him, watching. Ben was the one she had to convince now. Persuading them all to go to the dig was another matter. *Just go for it.*

As she approached, Ben stopped and looked at her. "What were you and my grandpa talking about?"

"He gave me this." She lifted the bag of gall medicine.

Ben set the brush down on a fencepost and pushed his hat back, revealing a furrowed brow. "What for?"

Anny took another deep breath. "The warrior from the legend has been appearing to me. Your grandpa said this will protect me if he's evil."

Ben's eyes widened. "The warrior? Where?"

Anny told him the whole story and signed her words so Eric could follow the conversation. "Eric was with me at the dig and Scout was with me at the school. They both know I'm telling the truth."

Ben looked at Eric and Scout.

"She is, Ben, I swear," said Eric.

"Yeah," agreed Scout. "I even walked up to the cafeteria windows waving at you and none of you saw me."

"Your grandpa says we're alike," Anny continued. "He sees things, too. He says people like us are special, even if white people don't think so."

Ben stared at her for a few moments. His gaze moved back to Eric, then to Scout, then back to her. He let out a long breath. "Well...if my grandpa believes you, and Eric and Scout do, then I guess I do, too...."

Anny didn't think he sounded so sure. She dismissed that for the moment. "We can prove Dr. Sanderson is guilty."

"How?" asked Scout.

"We should ride the horses over to the dig and snoop around. If Dr. Sanderson's hat doesn't have the headband on it, we'll know he's guilty."

"Oh, I don't know...," said Ben. "You guys don't really know how to ride. It could be dangerous."

"Now you sound like your uncle," Anny retorted in exasperation. "Don't you want Dr. Sanderson and Bill to go to jail if they started that fire?"

"Yeah."

"Look, Ben," said Scout. "What if you take the lead and we all follow? We do that when my troop goes riding. A lot of us are beginners. We all just walk the horses."

Ben thought for a moment. "Well, that might work."

"I know it will," said Anny.

Ben hesitated again, then said finally, "Oh, all right. But you have to follow me and promise not go faster than I do."

"We promise," said Anny, and Scout and Eric agreed.

When the horses were saddled, Scout put on her backpack.

"What do you need that for?" Ben chided. "We'll only be gone for a few hours. All we need is water."

"Girl Scout rules! I'm not going without it."

"Girl Scout rules!" Ben mimicked in a high-pitched nasal voice. Then he began to laugh.

Teasing was a side of Ben that Anny hadn't seen before. She wasn't sure she liked it. She and Scout could tease each other and that was okay, but she knew how it felt to be made fun of by other people, and she hated having her sister suffer that fate. "Hey, you guys," she said, interrupting Ben's laughter. "We have work to do."

Ben suddenly focused on her. "What do I tell my grandpa?" Then he answered his own question. "I guess I'll tell him we're going on a trail ride."

A short time later, their canteens filled and tied to their saddles, they were ready.

"Be careful," Mr. Roanhorse told them. "Don't go far. Remember, Grandson, Eric and Anny are tenderfeet."

"I know, Grandfather. We'll be real careful." Grabbing the horn, Ben swung smoothly into the saddle without even putting his foot in the stirrup.

"How did you do that?" Scout asked in astonishment.

Ben smiled. "Just practice."

Anny found herself wishing she had that ability. Picking up the reins, she patted Nugget's golden face, then kicked her slightly to get her moving.

After awhile, Ben said, "We'll never get there if the horses just walk. We have to trot. Can you handle that?"

"Yeah," said Anny, and the others agreed.

Ben kicked his horse's sides lightly. Anny, Scout, and Eric did likewise.

Anny practiced what she had been taught about sitting the saddle so she didn't bounce. It was almost as though her lower body detached itself from her upper body and moved with the motion of the horse. She was proud of herself; soon she didn't even have to hang on to the saddlehorn. *Nugget makes it easy, though.* She patted the mare on the shoulder. The horse was gentle and had a very smooth gait. Anny liked her a lot.

A few hours later, Ben stopped. "The dig is over that next hill. Let's find a place to tie the horses and sneak in on foot."

Anny wondered how Ben could possibly know where they were. Jim was right. The terrain looked all the same—just sandy desert, dotted with red rock formations and scrub brush in various shades of green and mountain ranges all along the horizon. They had ridden for a long time and didn't seem to be closer to anything. She trusted Ben, however, so she said, "I don't know where we should leave the horses, but I can show you a great place to sneak in. There's a path that leads right to the dig from behind a bunch of boulders."

"Okay," said Ben. "I just remembered a box canyon about half a mile from here. We can put the horses there."

Ben kicked his horse gently and once again they were off. Soon they reached the canyon. The entrance between the high cliffs was narrow, but as they rode through it, Anny saw there was a much wider area inside.

Ben dismounted. "Let's leave the horses here. We'll block the opening in case they get loose."

Anny and the others got off their horses, then helped Ben wedge a long, thick branch between some rocks.

Ben dropped his mare's reins over it. "This makes them think they're tied up. We can't really tie them up with those bridles on. It's too dangerous. They could cut their tongues if something scares them and they try to get away."

Anny followed Ben's lead, as did Eric and Scout, and when the horses were standing quietly, their cinches loosened so they could breath more easily, the kids gathered more poles and brush to block the canyon's entrance.

When they were done, Ben brushed dirt from his hands. "Scout, you'd better leave that backpack here."

"No way!"

"What if Dr. Sanderson sees us and we have to run? It will slow you down."

Reluctantly, Scout found a safe spot for her gear where the horses wouldn't trample it.

"Okay," said Ben. "I think we're ready to go."

Anny began to feel excited at the prospect of finally proving Dr. Sanderson had dug the holes at the school—and perhaps had started the fire—and was treasure-hunting. Finally, she saw the rock outcropping ahead. "There it is. Follow me."

She started up the narrow path between the rocks, stopping to point out the pictograph to Scout and Ben.

The gas cans still lay strewn all over the clearing.

"You're right, Anny," said Ben. "These wouldn't be here unless Dr. Sanderson was trying to hide them. They would be near his truck—or at least near the pit."

Pride swelled up in Anny. She had swayed Eric, then Scout, and now Ben over to her side. Mr. Roanhorse had been with her all along. Jim was the only one left. She was determined to find the proof to convince him she was right. "The path goes down into the dig right here." She pointed to the other opening between the rocks. "Sh-h-h. Be quiet."

She led the group through the rocks and down the other side of the stony path. At the bottom, she peered around the boulder. The truck stood close to where she was hiding. A ladder stuck out of the pit. She didn't think the two archaeologists were there, but every few seconds, she saw dirt fly out and land on the surface. "They're both digging," she told the others. "The hole looks a lot deeper now."

Scout moved closer to Anny. "What if Dr. Sanderson is wearing his hat? We'll have to go right up to the pit to have a look at it."

Anny thought a moment. "Let me check the truck first. Maybe it's there. You guys wait here. I'll be right back."

She crawled on her hands and knees from boulder to boulder around the edge of the rock outcropping. Then glancing back at the pit to make sure no one was climbing the ladder, she ran from the last rock across the open area to the passenger side of the truck, which faced away from the pit. Quickly she ducked down beside the door.

Anxiety swept over her, and she tried to fight it off. Slowly she stood up, then glanced into the truck's bed. Empty. Moving to the cab, she took a deep breath, then she peered into the door's open window and down at the torn, brown leather seat. There was no hat there, either, only some dirty, rumpled papers under a box of tissues. Disappointed, she almost turned away, still fighting the uneasy feelings, but something—a single phrase—caught her eye. She looked closer at the papers.

"...you'll have won."

Chapter 15

Reaching through the window, she moved the box of tissues and started reading at the top of the page. Chills ran up her spine.

There it was—in black and white! She almost hadn't seen it under the smudgy fingerprints that covered the paper.

> Look for the snowy peak so tall,
> Behind the open portal wall....

Dr. Sanderson had a copy of the poem! She finally had the proof of Dr. Sanderson's guilt that Jim couldn't ignore!

I'll bet that's what he and Bill were looking at out in front of the trading post. Maybe it's a fake, maybe there's no treasure, but Dr. Sanderson believes it's real. If he didn't, he wouldn't be digging here. Has he discovered its location?

Quickly she snatched the paper from the seat and ran back to where the others waited, trying to move over the well-worn path without making any noise. A feeling of elation swept over her. Once again, her perceptions had been validated. Knowing she wasn't alone in her differences was giving her confidence in who she was. At least she wasn't weird or crazy. There were others just like her, and Mr. Roanhorse was one of them. She could use her abilities to benefit people, the way Mr. Roanhorse had, but she would have to learn not to care what anyone else thought. Her heart sang at the prospects of what lay ahead, but she forced herself to focus on the here and now, to turn her attention back to the matter at hand.

"Look at this!" she whispered loudly, waving the paper. Then she thrust it toward Ben. "It's a copy of the poem! I found it on the truck seat!"

Ben took the paper and began to read, while Scout and Eric crowded over his shoulder.

"I don't believe it!" Scout exclaimed.

Lifting his gaze from the paper, Ben pushed his hat back on his head and sighed. "You were right about this, too. Dr. Sanderson and Bill *are* treasure-hunting."

"Wait til Jim sees this!" said Eric.

Ben folded the paper. "We have to get back to the hogan right away. My uncle will want to call the Tribal Police." He handed the poem back to Anny. "Keep this safe. We'll need it for evidence."

Ben sighed again as Anny slipped the paper deep into her pocket. "I just thought of something. If Dr. Sanderson or Bill notices that paper is gone, they'll know someone's on to them. I'd better make sure that old truck won't start anymore."

"That's risky," Anny said. "I was lucky they didn't see me...."

"But if they get away, the police will never find them. We have to do something."

"Anny's right," said Scout. "Won't that hood make noise when it goes up?"

"I won't open it, then. I'll crawl underneath and disable it from there."

"We'll go with you," said Anny. "We'll stay out of sight, and if Dr. Sanderson or Bill comes out of the pit, we'll yell to let you know."

Ben shook his head. "No, don't yell. Make an animal noise, like this." He cupped his hands over his mouth and made a soft cooing sound.

"I think I can do that," said Scout.

"Okay, we're set." Ben started down the narrow path, Anny right behind him. Ben stopped before the last large boulder and peeked around it. "They're still digging," he whispered.

"Hurry." Anny still wasn't convinced this was the right thing to do. She thought they should get the horses and head for the hogan, but she kept silent as Ben gave her his hat.

Crawling on his hands and knees behind the smaller rocks, he made his way to the side of the pickup as she had done moments before. Flattening himself out on the ground, he rolled underneath the truck between the sets of wheels.

Anny couldn't see what he was doing, but his feet stuck out the passenger side. Suddenly, an ominous feeling settled over her. She couldn't tell if it was from learning that Dr. Sanderson and Bill were up to no good after all or if Ben was in real danger.

From the corner of her eye, she saw movement at the edge of the pit. The ladder wobbled slightly, and a moment later,

Bill's head emerged above ground level. Anny gasped, then whispered to Scout, "The bird noise! The bird noise!"

Scout's eyes widened. She quickly cupped her hands over her mouth and made the cooing sound.

Ben didn't come out from under the truck, though Bill was standing beside the pit and holding the ladder. "Again!" Anny said, almost a little too loudly.

Scout repeated the bird call. Still Ben didn't move.

Dr. Sanderson's head poked out of the pit, his worn, brown hat firmly on his head. As Anny watched him talking to Bill, she squinted her eyes to see the crown. She saw only brown— no beads, no turquoise, no silver. She opened her mouth to tell Scout and Eric, but to her horror, the man's head turned toward the truck, and his eyes narrowed as he stared eye-level beneath it. "What the—!" he cried.

Ben rolled out from under the truck at last and stumbled clumsily back toward Anny, his hand over his eye.

Dr. Sanderson scrambled up the ladder. "Hey, you!"

"He's seen Ben!" Anny cried. "Run!"

The three almost fell over one another as they darted up the path, through the clearing with its empty gas cans, and down the other side of the rocks. They didn't stop running until they were back at the box canyon and safely concealed behind the bushes that blocked the narrow, high entrance.

Anny leaned against the canyon wall, gasping for breath, her heart pounding, beads of sweat dripping down her forehead. She glanced across to Scout and Eric, who were in no better shape.

When her heart stopped pounding, and her breathing was back under her own control, she peered through the pole and brush blockade to the reddish, flat desert beyond. Ben was nowhere in sight.

Chapter 16

Anny staggered to her feet. She tried to swallow, recoiling from the pain that action caused in her parched mouth. *"No!"* she cried to herself. Behind her, one of the horses snorted and stamped its hoof, but she barely heard it.

Scout, still gasping for breath, was suddenly beside her. "Where's—Ben? I thought—he was—with us."

"So did I," Anny whispered, leaning against the canyon wall for support. The smooth rock felt cool through her sweatshirt. "He must—still be—at the dig."

Scout's mouth fell open. "You mean—Dr. Sanderson—has him?"

Anny sank down on a rock. "What have I done? I should have made sure Ben was with us before I told you to run." She threw up her arms in despair. "This is all my fault!" She bent forward, burying her face in her hands. Then she felt a hand on her shoulder and looked up to see Eric. The comforting look on his face did nothing to calm her down.

Jumping up, she almost pushed him out of the way, waving her hands wildly. "It's my fault! I knew something bad was going to happen and I didn't tell Ben! If I had, he would be here with us now!" The words tumbled out, but even in her confusion, she saw Eric squinting at her lips.

"Stop!" he signed wildly. *"I can't understand you."*

Anny couldn't think. All she knew was that she had ignored the one thing she should have known was a sure sign of danger— that uneasy feeling. It wasn't just a neighbor's cat this time; it was a person's life in danger, a person who was close to her. *Some friend I am!* "I'm sorry," she said and signed. "I'm worried about Ben. This is all my fault."

"It's everyone's fault," Eric signed and spoke. "We never should have come out here without telling Mr. Roanhorse what we were really doing."

Taking a canteen from her horse's saddle, Scout unscrewed the lid, gulped from the spout, then handed it to Anny. "There's only one thing to do. Rescue him."

A wave of hope swept over Anny. "You're right! There are three of us and only two of them. We *can* rescue Ben. Let's go! We have to hurry!"

Scout held up her hand. "Wait a minute."

Anny stared at her. "What do you mean, 'Wait a minute'? We have to get him right now!"

"I mean we have to have a plan. And look at the sky."

Anny hadn't even noticed the red streaks crisscrossing the now grayish sky, and, far off on the horizon, the yellow ball that was the sun was only half visible above the mountaintops.

"It's going to be night soon," Scout continued. "We won't have any luck rescuing Ben after that. You know how dark it gets in the desert."

Eric's eyes went wide. "You want us to stay out here all night? *Alone?*" His voice was high-pitched.

Anny knew he was as scared as she was. "No way! We have to go get Jim and Mr. Roanhorse. They'll help us!"

"Do you know where the hogan is? Even my compass won't do us any good if we don't know which way to go."

Anny didn't answer, realizing her sister was absolutely right. Finally, she found her voice. "But we don't have any food and hardly any water. What are we going to eat? And it's cold out here!"

"And what about wild animals?" Eric shrieked.

Anny gasped. "Wild animals?"

"Yeah!" Eric continued. "Like mountain lions or bears!"

"Mountain lions are in the mountains, silly," said Scout, "and so are bears. And we aren't."

"What about coyotes?" said Eric.

"Probably," admitted Scout. "Look, I don't want to stay out here any more than you do, but the first rule of being lost is to stay right where you are. People will eventually find you. Once it gets dark, we won't be able to see a thing. We'll get lost ourselves. Then we won't have any chance of rescuing Ben *or* getting found. We just have to hope that Jim and Mr. Roanhorse can track us in the morning. In the meantime, we'll figure out a good plan to rescue Ben when the sun comes up."

"What if Dr. Sanderson and Bill hurt Ben?" Eric signed to Anny.

Chapter 17

"We have to rescue him first," Anny signed back. She peered out the canyon mouth but saw no movement beyond.

Scout knelt down and began rummaging through her backpack. "The horses need some water. I'll cup my hands. Can you pour water in from our canteens?"

When they finished watering the horses, Scout said, "Now we have to make a real camp."

"A real camp?" asked Anny.

"With fire, food, beds, and everything."

Anny looked around at the canyon floor and saw nothing but scrub brush and sand. "How?"

"You'll see." Scout stood up. "We'll make the fire first." She pointed to an open area. "That seems like a good spot. It's clear, and it's not within sight of the opening to the canyon. Dr. Sanderson and Bill can't see it." Picking up a stick, she drew a line, forming a circle about six feet across. "We have to clear away everything inside this line down to the dirt." She began picking up the dried leaves, grass, and brush from within the designated area.

Anny glanced at Eric, then shrugged and began to help.

When the ground within the circle was cleared down to its sandy base, Scout leaned over and picked up a large rock. "Now look for more of these."

Anny and Eric did as they were told, searching the canyon floor for the requested stones. As they brought them to the circle, Scout arranged them in a neat row around its rim.

When the rocks were in place, Scout put her hands on her hips, surveying their handiwork. "We're lucky it's not windy. A fire would be very hard to control. We should have a bucket of water and a shovel before starting it, in case we have to put it out, but this will have to do." She looked around and pointed to another area about fifteen feet away. "Now we need firewood. Let's put it over there."

Anny and Eric glanced at one another again. Though Anny never criticized her sister's scouting obsession, she had considered a lot of it useless. She was rapidly changing her mind. In fact, she found herself beginning to admire Scout's knowledge of how to survive in this wilderness. She didn't know the first thing to do, and from the look on Eric's face, he didn't, either.

"We need tinder, kindling, and fuel," her twin went on. She picked up debris from the ground. "This is tinder." She held out a skinny little twig about as thick as a match and the length of a new pencil. "And this is kindling." In her other hand was a thicker twig. "Anything up to the size of your thumb is fine, but be sure they're dry. You'll know they are if they snap when you break them." Looking around, she picked up a small log. "This is fuel."

The three set about gathering the firewood, piling it where Scout had indicated. When they were done, Scout picked some of the larger logs and set them in the middle of the stone circle. Laying two of the logs flat on the ground to form two sides of a triangle in the center of the firepit, she put a third one a little way up from the bottom to form an A. "This is called a Basic A fire."

Rising to her feet, she brushed off the knees of her pants, selected several handfuls of tinder from the woodpile, then placed a few on the crossbar of the A-shaped logs. She dropped the rest to the ground, reached into her backpack, pulled out a little box, then turned to Anny and Eric. "Before we light the fire, we have to agree on a few things. First of all, we can't ever leave the fire unattended or let it go out. Besides keeping us warm, the fire will keep any wild animals away. We have to take turns standing guard all night."

"We need to keep watch for Dr. Sanderson and Bill anyway," said Eric. "Let's draw straws to see who's first."

"Okay." Scout knelt down, withdrew a match from the box, and struck it. She let it burn for a few seconds, then moved it under the tinder. As the fire caught, she added more tinder. When it was burning briskly, she placed pieces of kindling in a crisscross formation over it, thick sticks at the bottom and smaller ones across the top. "This fire should burn steadily without much feeding. Now we need to make our beds."

"Beds?" Anny hadn't even thought of that. Then she groaned. "Oh, no! Our sleeping bags are still in the back of the station wagon!"

"If I'd been as careful as I should have, I would've at least brought mine," Scout said. "Well, we'll have to improvise." She gazed at the horses, who still stood "tied" to the pole Ben had placed on the ground. "We'll need those saddle blankets. The horses' fur will keep them warm."

Without a word, Eric and Anny followed Scout's lead in unsaddling their horses. Anny's admiration for her sister's ingenuity grew by the minute.

When they finished, Scout said, "We have to gather any soft grass we can find. Make a pile long and wide enough to sleep on to keep you off the cold ground. Then we'll use the saddle blankets as covers."

They set about this next task, and when they were finished, Scout announced, "*Now* we can eat."

She returned to her backpack and pulled out some chocolate bars. Holding them out, she said, "I know it seems selfish to eat when we don't know whether Ben will get any dinner, but we're not going to do him any good if we're too weak to rescue him. Make them last as long as you can."

Anny reached for one, knowing her sister was right.

Eric took one, too, ripping the paper off, then he stared at the backpack. "What else have you got in there?"

"Enough for breakfast, too."

Sitting cross-legged on folded-up saddle blankets by the warm, soft glow of the crackling fire, they ate their candy bars. Then Scout passed around the canteen again.

After his turn, Eric handed it back to Scout. "You've saved us! I'll never make fun of your Girl Scout stuff again, I swear!"

"He's right, Sis," added Anny. "You're great! We'd have been in real trouble without you!"

"Yeah, yeah," Scout retorted, but Anny could see the smile forming at the edges of her sister's mouth.

A short time later, Anny said and signed, "How are we going to rescue Ben?"

They stayed awake as long as they could discussing their ideas for their friend's rescue. They finally decided on what they thought was a foolproof plan. Anny offered to take the first shift watching the fire.

"I'll go second," said Eric. "After all Scout's done, she deserves to sleep the longest."

"Thanks." Scout stood up. "The fire's getting low." In the bright moonlight, Anny watched her sister retrieve an armload of kindling from the woodpile and add it carefully to the fire. "When it gets low again, add about the same amount of kindling as I just did."

Anny nodded, savoring the aroma of the burning wood and taking comfort in the fire's warmth.

"Wake me up when you need to sleep," Eric signed.

She nodded again as he and Scout lay down on the beds of grass, covering themselves with the saddle blankets.

"Eewwww!" Eric cried. "This stinks of horse sweat!"

Anny and Scout laughed, then Anny turned her attention to the fire. Shortly, she heard deep breathing. Scout and Eric were asleep, and she suddenly felt very alone. *What if wild animals aren't afraid of fire? What if I accidentally fall asleep? What if Dr. Sanderson takes Ben someplace where we will never find him?* The best plan in the world wouldn't help then. She pulled her knees up, wrapping her arms around them.

A mournful howl broke the stillness. *A coyote,* she thought. She had heard plenty of them in the hills behind her family's house in California.

Something scurried through the nearby bushes. Anny swallowed, trying to ignore it. She turned her thoughts to her parents and how angry they would be when they found out about this disaster. She could just hear them. *"What have you done now?"* She—and Scout, too, no doubt—would be grounded for life and never allowed to take a trip alone again.

Out of the corner of her eye, she detected movement across the campfire. Through the flames, she saw him, sitting cross-legged on the ground just outside the stone rim of the firepit. He was closer to her than he had ever been, and he watched her intently through the firelight. His black hair flowed over his coppery shoulders, the brightly colored feathers that hung from the dark strands plainly visible. His hands rested on his thighs, and a slight smile crossed his lips. The medallion hung around his neck. Anny tried to see the design on it but couldn't. Behind him, his horse stood silently.

She wondered why she felt no fear of sitting across a campfire from a ghost, why she was bathed in a warm, comfortable sensation instead. *Would I feel that if he were an evil spirit?* She fingered the pouch of gall medicine at her throat. Perhaps the warrior needed her help for something, and he knew that right now she, Scout, Eric, and Ben needed his help, and he had come to offer it.

Maybe I'm being stupid. I know nothing about him. He might be tricking me into believing he's good. Maybe the gall medicine is the only thing saving me. I'll trick him right back. She smiled, hoping he would believe she thought he was her friend. She wondered if she should even try to sleep. Eric and Scout couldn't see the ghost, and if he harmed them, she would never forgive herself. She couldn't take the risk. She had to stay awake all night.

Despite her best intentions, her eyelids became heavy, and she slumped sideways as sleep tried to claim her. When she couldn't stay awake another second, she forced herself to get Eric. Kneeling beside him, she shook him gently until he finally opened his eyes and sat up.

"Is it time already?" he signed.

When she was sure he was wide awake, she told him about the warrior, who still sat quietly beside the fire.

Eric stared at her, then taking a deep breath, he crawled out of his sleeping bag. *"Don't worry. I'll watch things for the rest of the night. Let Scout sleep."*

Anny knew Eric was being brave for her sake and Scout's. She felt guilty thinking about going to sleep and leaving him alone with the ghost, and she told him so.

He stood up. *"I'll be fine. If he wanted to hurt us, he would have by now."* He paused. *"Wouldn't he...?"*

"I don't know...." Anny was angry with herself for not being able to determine what the ghost wanted, and she wonder-ed if Eric should wear her gall medicine while he stood guard.

"No, you keep it," he signed when she asked him.

"Wake me up if you need to." She collapsed onto her saddle blanket, barely able to crawl underneath.

It seemed only a minute later that Scout shook her awake. The first rays of sun peeked over the gray horizon as birds chirped softly from high up on the canyon wall.

An image of the warrior flashed into her mind, and she jumped up, throwing the saddle blanket aside.

"What's the matter?" said Scout, rising to her feet.

"I have to check on Eric." Hugging herself against the chill of the early morning air, she saw him sitting by the brightly burning fire, warming his hands. She sighed with relief. The warrior and his horse were gone. She wondered how long they had stayed.

"Eric should have woken me up," said Scout. "I would have taken a turn."

"You did enough last night. You deserved to sleep." Anny felt grubby and her mouth tasted as though she hadn't brushed her teeth in days. She tried to ignore her desire to step into a nice, warm shower by helping Scout and Eric pour sand over the fire to put it out. At the same time, she took advantage of the opportunity to search the other side of the campfire for the warrior's footprints and his horse's hoofprints. She found nothing—no trace that anyone other than the three of them had been in the canyon. Despite what Mr. Roanhorse said, she wanted real proof that she wasn't just hallucinating, after all.

"We have to pour sand on the fire and make sure not even one ember is still glowing," Scout told her and Eric. "The fire could start burning again. That's why we could use that bucket of water and a shovel. There can't be any trace of our having been here."

When the fire was out, the rocks scattered, and the area returned to the way they had found it, they saddled the horses. It was time to put their plan into action. They had debated leaving the horses behind in the canyon, but if they needed to run again, having the horses nearby for a quick getaway was safer than trying to outrun two grown men. One of them was bound to get caught. Then they would have two people to rescue instead of one. That Dr. Sanderson and Bill might see them riding to the dig was worth the risk.

Eric removed the blockade from the canyon entrance. He mounted his horse, then grabbed the reins to Ben's.

"Ready?" Anny asked Scout and Eric when they were on their horses.

"Yes," they answered.

Anny pressed her heels slightly into Nugget's side. "Okay. Let's go." She took one last long look around in case the warrior and his horse had reappeared. She saw nothing. *We really need your help now.*

Chapter 18

Anny gripped the reins as they rode across the sandy desert in the cool morning air. The sun was still barely over the horizon. She wished Ben were here to lead them.

Despite the chilly temperature, beads of sweat formed on her brow and ran down her face. *If they've hurt Ben....* From their discussions the night before, she knew Scout and Eric shared her fear. Perhaps they had forced Ben to fix the truck. They might even have left and taken him with them. *Then what will we do?*

Stopping just behind the rock outcropping, they dismounted, dropping their horses' reins into some scrub brush.

"I hope Ben was right when he said the horses'll think they're tied up like this," said Anny, as Nugget shook her head, stamped her hoof, and snorted. Anny's gaze darted around. "I hope those guys didn't hear that!"

"Yeah," said Scout, quietly removing the long, coiled rope from Ben's saddle.

They stood very still, waiting to see if anyone came. No one did. After what seemed an eternity, when they still had heard and seen nothing, they started up the narrow trail.

Once again they went through the clearing, past the empty gas cans, and around the rocks, Anny in the lead. She stopped at the last boulder, rested her hands on the cool gray stone, and carefully peered around it to the dig. The old blue truck still sat parked in the same place. Dr. Sanderson and Bill, hatless, dressed in sweatshirts and jeans, were moving around next to the pit. She sighed with relief as her heart began to pound.

Eric touched her shoulder. *"Do you see Ben?"*

Her gaze darted around. Across the dig, he sat with his back against a large rock. Thick, white rope bound his hands and feet, and a white cloth gagged his mouth. *"He's tied up on the other side of the pit."*

Suddenly Anny realized what the archaeologists were doing. They were gathering their tools and supplies and placing them in a pile. "Looks like they're getting ready to leave, but how can they when their truck doesn't work?"

"Sh-h-h-h! They'll hear you!" Scout whispered.

As Anny watched the men, she chastised herself for nearly giving away their location, but the archaeologist and his assistant continued working. She sighed with relief. They hadn't heard her.

"We'd better put our plan into action," Scout continued.

"Okay. You and Eric go around the other side of the rocks. Come into the pit the way we planned."

Scout nodded, and she and Eric started down the trail.

Anny closed her eyes a moment. *Could this plan really work?* Her heart still pounding and her palms sweaty, she crouched quietly against the boulder until she heard Scout's now familiar bird call signaling that she and Eric were ready. She bolted into action, running out into the open and shouting at Dr. Sanderson and Bill as loudly as she could. The men wheeled around, startled, and stared briefly before dropping their tools to the ground. At that same instant, Scout and Eric, each holding an end of the long rope, ran toward them. The men wheeled again.

Anny held her breath. Out of nowhere, the warrior and his horse appeared right behind Scout and Eric, galloping at full speed toward them.

Chapter 19

It all happened so fast, Anny stood dumbfounded, unable to move. The apparition and his horse charged right through her sister and Eric and straight for Dr. Sanderson and Bill. The two men let out bloodcurdling screams and stumbled backwards as the warrior headed right for them. Scout and Eric kept running, and before the rope made contact with the two men's bodies, they had fallen, arms flailing, into the pit. The warrior and horse galloped over the hole and faded away.

Scout and Eric quickly pulled the ladder from the pit, hauled it several yards away, and dropped it on the ground. "It worked! Our plan worked!" Scout shouted. They both jumped up and down as they gazed into the deep hole.

"Mm-mm! Mm-mm!"

Ben's muffled cries finally registered, and Anny rushed to his side. Dr. Sanderson and Bill shouted back at them as Anny frantically worked to untie the gag over Ben's mouth.

As soon as it was off, he cried, "I thought you guys would never come!"

Anny began to loosen the ropes around his hands. "You thought we'd leave you here?"

"I thought maybe you tried to go for help and got lost." His hands free, Ben quickly untied the rope around his ankles, then got to his feet, using the rock for support. "Ooo-hh, I'm stiff from sitting all night."

Eric and Scout rushed to them, ignoring the archaeologists' demands for help.

"Hey, Ben!" said Eric. "We're so glad you're all right."

"What a great plan!" exclaimed Ben. "How did you ever think of it?"

"We weren't sure it would work," said Scout, "but luck was with us!"

Anny wondered about that. Had the men been frightened by Scout and Eric running at them or had the phantom revealed himself long enough to scare them into falling into the pit? She had thought the rider was going to run down her sister and Eric, but he had galloped right through them. Confused, she decided to say nothing, not wanting to take this moment away from Scout or Eric. No one ever needed to know of the warrior's involvement, even if he was the real hero. "What happened, anyway?" she said instead.

Ben sighed in exasperation. "I drained the oil out. Some of it fell in my eye. I couldn't see. Dumb, huh?"

"We need to get back to the hogan. We have to tell Jim so he can call the Tribal Police." Anny said this last sentence loud enough that she hoped the two men would hear her over their shouting.

"Wait! I'm starving!" Ben began to rummage through the supplies. "These guys didn't give me anything to eat!"

"We're starving, too!" Scout helped Ben search, and soon they discovered a loaf of bread and some crackers.

Anny took two slices of bread. "Let's eat it on the way. These guys'll be safe til we get back."

"We can't leave them here with no water," said Scout.

"Whaddaya mean?" protested Ben. "They didn't give me any to drink!"

"Just the same, two wrongs don't make a right."

"What about the horses?" Ben continued. "Have they had any water?"

"They drank some from the canteens," said Scout.

"They need more than that. We'll take them to the creek."

Scout hunted through the pile, retrieved a canteen, and gave it a shake. Liquid sloshed inside. "This one is nearly full." Over Ben and Eric's protests, she dropped it down to the men. "We'll take the rest for the horses til we get to the creek."

"If you know what's good for you," snarled Dr. Sanderson, "you'll put that ladder back in here right now!"

"Let's go," Scout said, over the shouts of Dr. Sanderson and Bill.

A few hours later, Anny spotted the hogan in the distance. Jim's red pickup was parked in front, and as they drew closer, Anny saw two figures, one in denim-colored clothes and one in a red shirt. *Jim and Mr. Roanhorse*, she thought. The one in denim, obviously Jim, noticed them and jumped into the cab of the truck. Anny heard a low hum as the engine started. The pickup lurched backwards, then forward, as Jim turned onto the road and headed in their direction.

When the truck got close, Jim braked hard and jumped out. "Where in the world have you been?" he cried. "The Tribal Police and I have been searching all night!"

"We're fine, thanks to Scout," Anny assured him. "We're sorry we worried you." The story spilled from them all at once.

The big man put up his hands. "Hold it! One at a time!"

Quickly, Anny relayed the whole story, ending with how they had trapped Dr. Sanderson and Bill in the pit while rescuing Ben. "And now the police have to arrest them!"

Jim stared at her in amazement and he was silent a moment. Then he shook his head. Anny's heart sank; he couldn't possibly think she was making this up—*could he?*

The science teacher let out a long sigh. "I don't know what to say except I'm sorry I didn't believe you sooner. All of this could have been avoided." He opened the truck door. "Let's get back to the hogan and put those horses up. The police should be back any minute." He hopped into the cab, pulled the door shut, then said through the open window, "We'll call your parents later." He turned the vehicle around and drove back to the hogan, dust clouds billowing behind him.

The prospect of their parents' learning about their dangerous adventure was diminished by Anny's pride she had finally convinced Jim that Dr. Sanderson and Bill were bad men.

As they approached the hogan, Mr. and Mrs. Roanhorse rushed to them. Mrs. Roanhorse's silver concho necklace bounced back and forth as she shook her fist at Ben and scolded him in Navajo. They unsaddled the horses, and Anny told Mr. Roanhorse what had happened. Then she took him aside and explained the role the warrior had played. "He doesn't seem evil. He helped us."

The old man nodded. "I think he did help you, but we still don't know what he really wants. If he is a skinwalker, it is very dangerous to have contact with him. Do not be too quick to trust him."

Anny fingered the gall medicine around her neck. "I know this protected me. Thanks again for giving it to me."

Mr. Roanhorse nodded again. "And I did so just in time."

No sooner had they turned the horses loose in the corral when a white car bounced over the dirt trail leading to the hogan. Anny recognized the emblem on the door as that of the Tribal Police.

"Here's John Yazzie," said Jim. "He's the officer who's been helping me look for you."

The car pulled to a stop and the engine shut off. A muscular man in a brown uniform stepped out. "*Ya e'eh tey,*" he said to Mr. and Mrs. Roanhorse, who returned the greeting. "Glad to see you kids are back. Are you all right? What happened?"

Quickly, Anny and the others repeated their story.

"Sure does sound as though they're up to no good," agreed the officer. "You say they're still in the pit?"

"Yes!" exclaimed Anny. "We have to get back there!"

"Show me where it is."

"I'll take Ben in my truck and the others can ride with you, if it's okay," said Jim.

"Sure." The police officer held open the back door of the squad car. "Hop in, kids."

At the dig. the officer parked behind the rock outcropping so they could walk up the path. In the clearing, he slowly circled the cans, studying them. "Mighty suspicious, all right...."

"I think they were used to set the fire," said Anny.

They continued down the path towards the dig. Anny immediately noticed how quiet it was. She didn't hear the archaeologists shouting. *Maybe they gave up since no one could hear them*, she thought, ignoring the familiar uneasiness creeping over her once again.

As they rounded the last boulder, Anny stopped, staring in disbelief. The blue truck was nowhere in sight, and the top of the ladder stuck out of the pit. Her eyes darted around, looking for any sign of the pickup. She rushed forward with the others to the pit and looked in. *Empty!* Dr. Sanderson and Bill were gone!

Chapter 20

"They were right here!" Anny couldn't understand it.

Scout threw her arms up in the air in exasperation. "Eric and I pulled that ladder out and dumped it way over there! There's no way it could have gotten back into the pit!"

"And I let all the oil out of their truck," cried Ben. "There's no way they could drive it! And that big pile of stuff's gone!"

Removing his sunglasses, Officer Yazzie squinted as he studied the abandoned dig. Then putting on his glasses again, he hooked his thumbs in his belt and shifted his weight to one leg. "One must have stood on the other's shoulders to get out. And they must have had some spare cans of oil."

"Spare cans?" Ben's gaze darted around. "I didn't see any!"

"They could have been in that big pile," said Jim.

"They wouldn't have been stupid enough to leave on foot, especially if they had a lot of equipment," the officer said.

"They'll get away!" Anny protested. "Can't we do *something*?"

"I'll radio in for everyone to be on the lookout for them," Officer Yazzie said, "but no doubt they're clear out of the state by now." He headed back toward the rock outcropping.

"There isn't anything else we can do here," said Jim. "We might as well go home."

On the verge of tears, Anny let out a long sigh. Despite all their efforts, their plan had failed. It had seemed so foolproof! But they hadn't thought of Dr. Sanderson having spare cans of oil. *Where was the warrior?* she wondered, as they walked to the car. *Why hadn't he stopped the men a second time?* She climbed into the squad car, leaning against the door as the car rumbled over the dirt track back to the highway.

After stopping at the hogan to get their gear and apologize again for worrying the Roanhorses, they headed back to Jim's in the station wagon. The trip seemed long and Anny was glad. All she wanted to do was think. Laying her head back on the smooth vinyl with her eyes closed gave her the chance. No one else said anything, either. All she heard in the quiet stillness of the desert morning was the fwop, fwop, fwop of the tires as the old car rolled along the long stretch of open road.

Jim finally broke the silence. "I know you're all disappointed that Dr. Sanderson and Bill got away, but don't worry. Officer Yazzie is one of the best. He and the other Tribal Police will track them down in no time."

What if they don't? They'll get away with the fire, treasure-hunting, and holding Ben hostage.

"You kids don't know how lucky you are," Jim went on. "You could have been seriously hurt if those men are as dangerous as they seem." He paused, shaking his head. "I just don't understand how archaeologists from the university.... It doesn't make sense...."

Anny knew Jim was trying to make them feel better. He could have lectured them again for being so stupid and reminded them how hard it would be for him to talk to their parents, but he didn't. She knew that talk would come, but she was grateful Jim was refraining from it now.

When the science teacher finally pulled into the driveway, Anny suddenly realized just how much she wanted to hop into a nice, warm shower. Having clean hair and a clean body had never been more appealing. "I have first dibs on the bathroom!" she shouted, racing past everyone to the front door.

Dressed in fresh jeans and a t-shirt, she returned to the living room. Eric was at the kitchen table playing a game of solitaire. Anny dropped into a chair across from him. *"Now that Jim believes us that Dr. Sanderson and Bill are treasure-hunting, we need to get him to help us find it before they do."*

"How? We don't even know where to begin looking."

She pointed to the painting of Window Rock over the living room couch, where Ben sat reading. The sun shone overhead. "When the sun shines o'er the circle round...," she said aloud as she signed the words.

Jim dropped his jean jacket on the couch and stopped beside them. "Window Rock can't be what the poem is talking about. There aren't any mountains right behind it. Monument Valley has lots of those formations, but I think the poem is talking about another one in the mountains several hours from here." He paused, scratching his chin. "But I don't remember any caves up there." He threw up his arms. "Will you listen to me? I sound like the treasure's really out there!"

"Can we go look?" Anny held her breath.

Ben dropped his book and jumped up. "Yeah! Can we?"

Jim glanced at both of them. "Dr. Sanderson and Bill could still be around. We sure don't want to run into them."

"But Officer Yazzie said they'd be out of the state by now," Ben protested.

"Yeah!" added Anny. "They wouldn't be stupid enough to stick around and risk getting arrested for kidnapping."

Jim sighed. "I'm sure you're right." He was silent a moment. "If the Tribal Council okays it, we'll go. Promise me you won't get your hopes up, okay?"

Anny and Ben cheered, and she signed Jim's words for Eric. Anny knew the treasure was out there. She could feel it right through to her bones. "Can we go today?"

Jim rubbed his hands together. "Why not? We can make a camping trip out of it. We'll stay overnight so we can look tomorrow, too. Most of your gear is still in the car, so while I make this call, get anything else you need. I'll get the food together."

Anny ran to the bathroom to fill in Scout, then listened as Jim called the Tribal Council and explained that they wanted to finish decoding the poem.

"I know it's just an old legend," he told the person at the other end, "but it will be fun for the kids." He paused. "Yes, we promise we won't touch anything we find."

After Anny dried her hair and the boys finished taking showers, Anny took a minute to turn on her laptop and write a quick note in her journal.

Can you believe I'm not crazy, after all? And I have my sister back! Mr. Roanhorse says my visions are real—that I have a special gift. Now almost everyone here believes me. Jim still doesn't know about my visions, though. Will I ever convince Mom and Dad? I shouldn't worry about that right now, though, because we're finally going treasure-hunting!

Soon they were rumbling down the highway in the warm sun once again. Anny sat in the back seat of the station wagon behind Jim, her heart singing. "We're going to look for treasure! We're going to look for treasure!"

As she daydreamed of finding the lost fortune, Jim said, "We'll have to stop at the trading post for more gas and supplies, but we can still get to the mountains in plenty of time before it gets dark."

A short time later, the tires of the old station wagon once again crunched across the gravel parking area of the trading post, and Jim stopped alongside the one lone gas pump. "Might as well gas up while we're here."

As they piled out of the car, Anny said, "I think I'll buy that bracelet I saw last time." She signed the words for Eric.

"Maybe I should get a souvenir for my grandma," he said.

"Yeah! Something besides that yo-yo!" Ben teased.

"We should get souvenirs for everyone, too," Anny said to her sister. She rushed past the shelves of dolls and pottery and the stacks of colorful woven blankets to the glass case holding the jewelry and stopped short. The silver bracelet with the turquoise stone and zigzag designs carved on the band was gone.

122

In its place was a clay medallion on a leather string. Carved in its center was a large thunderbird. "No way! That's just like the warrior's!" Wondering if its presence was more of the warrior's magic, she knew she had to have it. *Does his have a thunderbird in the center, too?* she wondered. She ran her hands over her pants pockets. "Darn! I left my money in my backpack."

"The car's unlocked," said Jim. He handed some cash to the woman at the counter.

"I'll be right back," she said over her shoulder, as she headed for the front door.

Opening the tailgate of the station wagon, she pulled out her backpack. She had just lifted the top flap when she heard tires crunch gravel. Looking up, she saw a white SUV driving up to the trading post.

She started rummaging through her backpack, then froze. Hadn't Ben's Aunt Elaine said Dr. Sanderson was coming to the Navajo Nation in his new, white SUV? Slowly she turned, then moved enough to see the back of the vehicle. It had only cardboard license plates with the car dealer's name.

The driver's door opened, and a tall, slim, elderly man in a blue plaid shirt and jeans stepped from the cab. With his neatly trimmed beard and gold-rimmed glasses, he looked like what her father would call "distinguished." The man turned his back to her and reached for something in the front seat.

Eric emerged from the trading post. He had obviously noticed her gaping at the man, for he glanced from one to the other. *"What is it? What's wrong?"*

She ran up onto the boardwalk beside him. *"Ben's aunt said Dr. Sanderson was coming to the Navajo Nation in his new, white SUV. Look at that SUV."*

The man stood up, put on an old, brown cowboy hat, closed the driver's door, and headed up the wooden steps.

Anny quickly moved to block his way. "Who *are* you?" she demanded.

Though the brim of his hat cast a shadow over his face, Anny could see his furrowed brow and startled expression as he stared at her. "I'm Philip Sanderson. Just who are you?"

Chapter 21

Anny stared right back. "*You're* not Philip Sanderson!" she snapped. "We know Philip Sanderson and you're not him!" She surprised herself with the harshness of her tone. She wasn't normally so outspoken.

With a rough, weathered hand, the man pushed his hat back on his head. Thick, white hair tumbled down over his forehead. "Young lady, whatever you're up to, I don't find it in the least bit funny." He started up the steps again. "Now please let me by."

"No!" A burst of shivers ran up Anny's spine, and she stood her ground, arms outstretched to block his way. "You helped them get away, didn't you? It was *you!*"

"What in the world is going on out here?" Jim asked from behind her as he stepped out onto the porch.

Feeling the safety of his presence, she pointed to the stranger. "He says he's Philip Sanderson!"

Scout and Ben crowded in the doorway of the trading post, their mouths open.

Jim's eyes narrowed as he studied the man. "Is that so?" He paused. "*Dr. Philip Sanderson?*"

125

"I assure you that's who I am," the stranger replied, "but it's really none of your business."

Ben moved out onto the porch and in front of Anny. "If you're Dr. Sanderson, then who's that other guy?"

"What other guy?" The man seemed genuinely confused.

"The Dr. Sanderson who's been working a dig over near Calico Mesa," said Jim.

The man's eyes widened. "What?"

"He claims he's Dr. Philip Sanderson," Jim repeated. "And his assistant, Bill, is working with him."

The man frowned. "What do they look like?"

"That Dr. Sanderson looks just like you, as a matter of fact," said Jim. "Right down to the plaid shirt and jeans."

"And the other one has scraggly brown hair," added Anny. "He's short and fat with a big scar running down his cheek."

The man took off his hat, pulled a white handkerchief from his shirt pocket, and wiped his forehead. "I should have known something like this might happen."

"Something like what?" Scout demanded.

The supposed Dr. Sanderson didn't answer but removed a brown leather wallet from his back pocket. Flipping it open, he took out a card and handed it to Jim. "My driver's license. Only because someone may be impersonating me."

Jim took the plastic card and studied it, then glanced at the man and back to the license. "Philip Sanderson, all right," he said finally. "You don't mind if the kids see for themselves, do you?"

Anny quickly signed to Eric to fill him in.

126

"No, I guess not," the archaeologist replied.

Jim handed the license to Anny as Eric and Ben moved beside her to look over her shoulder.

"How do we know it's not a phony?" said Ben. "I've seen on TV how people can get counterfeit ones."

"I can tell you I've been teaching archaeology at UA for the past thirty-five years," the man said. "I'm now the department head. My secretary is Joan Rodriguez."

"All information you could have gotten from the University of Arizona website," said Jim. "We'll need a little more."

The stranger sighed. "How about the fact that I'm on the Intercultural Affairs Committee?"

Jim ignored that. "Who heads the Biology Department?"

"Susan Teller," the man answered without hesitation. "She and I go way back. We went to college and then grad school together at Berkeley."

"He's for real," said Jim. "I went to UA myself. No way he'd know Susan Teller went to Berkeley unless he knew her."

"Couldn't he have gotten that from the website, too?" Anny asked, her suspicions still not completely allayed.

"Yes, but why would he? He would have reason to know about the Archaeology Department, but nothing else."

"I don't know...." Anny studied the man as she handed the license to Scout.

"Why don't you call UA and ask?" suggested the man.

Ben eyed the new vehicle with its cardboard tags. "Aunt Elaine did say the real Dr. Sanderson was coming here in a new, white SUV...."

"I know," Anny answered, as Ben and Eric studied the man's license. Convinced at last, she took the plastic card from them and handed it back to Dr. Sanderson, embarrassed now at how she had treated him. "I'm sorry."

"Apology accepted." The man slid the license into his wallet and returned it to his pocket. "Those men sound like Dutch Turner and Leroy Ferguson, two unsavory types from the San Francisco area. They came to see me at the university about helping them find a treasure they'd heard about."

"The Lost Treasure of the Golden Sun!" Anny exclaimed.

"You know about that?" He paused. "Perhaps you'd better tell me everything."

Anny and Jim related the entire story of the imposter and his "assistant," explaining how they had met them after the fire at the school and how Anny had discovered the gas cans when they visited the two at the dig. Anny told him about her suspicions that the men had set the fire while looking for the fortune, about finding the poem on the Internet, and how her suspicions about the men were proven when she found the same poem on the front seat of the old pickup. She deliberately avoided any mention of the warrior.

"They showed me that poem," said Dr. Sanderson. "Turner and Ferguson discovered it on the Internet, as you did, and wanted to come with me on this trip to look for the treasure. I told them it was just a legend, but they didn't believe me. When I refused to help, they became very angry. They must have found out my trip had been postponed. That gave them the perfect chance to come here on their own."

"You should know they're dangerous," said Jim. "They held my nephew hostage when the kids figured out what they were really up to."

Ben gave him the details on his capture while Scout and Eric told him about their nervewracking night in the desert.

"I'm very sorry for what you've been through," said Dr. Sanderson, "but I don't know if I can do anything to help you or the police find them."

"You can help us find that treasure, though," said Anny. "Then we can give it to Mrs. Nakai to rebuild the school."

"Like I said, that's just an old legend."

"That's what I told the kids," said Jim, "but Anny has done a good job decoding the poem, and the kids will have fun following the clues to see if anything is there."

"Yeah!" Anny agreed. For all his doubting, Jim was now solidly on her side. "We think the golden sun in the poem is the one on the Magic Rock and that the treasure is wherever that rock came from."

"The Magic Rock?" Dr. Sanderson said. "You mean the one I brought to Tribal Headquarters years ago?"

"*You're* the one who found the Magic Rock?" exclaimed Ben.

"Well, an old pothunter found it."

"What's a pothunter?" asked Anny.

"Someone who illegally hunts for pottery and other objects of historical value. He found it in a cave and wanted to sell it for a lot of money. But his truck broke down, and some Navajos found him wandering in the desert, half-crazed."

129

"The warrior did that!" cried Anny before she could stop herself, and she felt Scout's elbow jab her side.

"The warrior?" Dr. Sanderson asked, confused. "No, it was sunstroke, I'm sure."

Anny was relieved. She didn't want Dr. Sanderson thinking she was crazy, after all.

"How did you get the rock?" asked Ben.

"The pothunter couldn't remember where that cave was. Some Navajos brought the rock to me, hoping I could find its original location. Much as I tried, I couldn't, so I brought it to Tribal Headquarters. The Tribal Council put it in the school."

"That's how it got there, then," said Jim.

"We're on our way to the mountains to look for the treasure," explained Scout.

"Where in the mountains?"

"Near a formation I know that may be the one described in the poem," said Jim.

"Then it isn't Window Rock, like Turner and Ferguson claimed," said Dr. Sanderson. "I didn't think it was. I know the one you mean. That's near where I searched, but I obviously didn't look hard enough."

"Will you help us?" asked Anny. "Will you take us to where you were looking before?"

Chapter 22

"The Tribal Council gave us permission to go there so long as we don't touch anything," said Jim. " They think it's just an old legend, too."

The archaeologist looked at them a moment.

Anny held her breath waiting for his answer. With his help, they might find the treasure even faster.

Finally, he said, "Since it's okay with the Tribal Council, I will. As you said, it might be fun to see if that poem points to a real place. I have everything I need in my truck except the supplies I planned to get here. Give me fifteen minutes."

Anny took the opportunity to buy the medallion, which she immediately hung around her neck. Then she went back outside to wait with the others.

Dr. Sanderson soon emerged from the trading post, arms full of grocery bags. Setting them on the ground beside his SUV, he opened the door to the cab, reached inside, and brought out a folded road map. He opened it as he walked toward them. Then he laid it out on the hood of the station wagon and pointed to a spot on it. "We're here." He moved his hand a few inches over. "The cave is here."

Anny had a sudden thought. "Where's the dig?"

Jim pointed to another spot. "Right about here."

"And your dad's hogan?"

"Right here." He paused a moment. "That's odd. All those places form a straight line."

"That's where I saw the pictographs of the golden sun and the warrior. Near the hogan and by the dig."

"What are the first few lines of that poem again?"

Anny knew the poem by heart. "Look for the snowy peak so tall, Behind the open portal wall. When the sun shines o'er the circle round, lines you'll draw, then you'll have found, the warrior at his secret lair."

"I'll bet if you draw a line to the sun overhead from the rock formation," said Eric, "the line making it a right angle to the mountains from that snowy peak will point to where the treasure is."

"Absolutely right," said Jim. "Good job!"

"That's about where I tried to return the Magic Rock," said Dr. Sanderson. "We should look in the cave area first."

A short time later, the station wagon once again rolled down the highway, Dr. Sanderson and his SUV in the lead. Eventually the flatness of the desert and the straightness of the highway gave way to mountainous terrain and winding roads. Anny marveled at the change of scenery.

Dusk fell as Dr. Sanderson pulled off the road a few hours later and onto a dirt track leading into the woods. The old station wagon's tires spun as it bounced and jolted over the wide trail, and, as usual, Anny clung to the armrest for support.

"Slow down!" Jim grumbled. "This thing isn't four-wheel drive."

Finally, they stopped in a clearing. Dr. Sanderson stepped out of his truck and came up to the driver's side of the car as Jim rolled down the window.

"The cave is very near here," he said. "This will make a good place to camp."

Scout, Anny, and Eric built a fire.

"I'm certainly impressed," Jim told them as he surveyed their handiwork. "I would think that your troop leader would be, too, Scout."

Scout smiled. "Thanks."

They laughed and talked as they unpacked the car, shaking out their sleeping bags and placing them in a circle around the firepit. Anny put hers next to her sister's.

Soon they were sitting on logs in the warm glow of the fire, roasting hot dogs and corn on the cob, and finishing with s'mores for dessert. Jim told stories of his boyhood, of moving the sheep from the winter hogan between the red mesas, where his father and mother were now, to the summer hogan in the mountains. As he spoke, Anny recalled sitting by the glowing fire at the Roanhorses', and she could literally feel the warmth of the sheepskins as Jim told of huddling inside on a snowy night, could almost feel the cool desert floor as he talked of sitting among the yellow dogwood and cactus blooms on a warm summer day.

Jim stood up, brushing dirt from the back of his Levis. "How about we hit the hay so we can get an early start?"

This night, Anny was eager to go to bed. She crawled inside her sleeping bag, pulled the top up to her chin, and fell asleep as visions of lost treasure peppered her dreams.

A gentle breeze blew across Anny's face, and her eyes fluttered open to the first rays of sunlight. Birds chirped high up in the trees. She sat up and looked around. Everyone was still sound asleep. Quietly fishing her favorite red sweatshirt out of her backpack, she changed in her sleeping bag.

She got up, hugging her arms around herself in the chilly air. Now that she could study her surroundings in the light of day, she noticed the trail continued on beyond the other side of the clearing. Curious, she decided to take a short walk to see if she could spot the cave. She quickly pulled on her hiking boots, telling herself that as long as she kept to the trail, she wouldn't get lost.

Grabbing her jacket from her backpack, she put it on and started on her way, kicking at pebbles as she walked. Tall pine trees stretched their branches over the trail, and she couldn't help but feel a little like Gretel from the old fairy tale. Unlike Gretel and her brother, though, she wasn't lost.

She walked for almost ten minutes and was surprised when she felt the familiar uneasiness return. She tried to ignore it. *There isn't anything wrong*, she told herself. When she rounded a bend in the trail, she stopped short and gasped. There, between some dense trees, was a low opening in the rocks that had to be the cave. In front of it, leaning against a large boulder and staring off in the other direction, was *Leroy Ferguson!*

134

Anny darted behind a tree, pressing herself against its rough bark. She peered around the thick trunk, angry with herself for wearing her red sweatshirt. She was lucky the man hadn't seen her. He turned, and glancing around, ducked his head and disappeared inside the cave.

Dr. Sanderson had lied to them, she suddenly realized. He *was* involved with the two treasure-hunters. He had led her and the others right into a trap!

Chapter 23

Anny waited a few minutes. When no one came back out, she bolted from behind the tree and ran as fast as she could back down the trail.

The camp was alive with activity as she came within view. She wanted to walk so Dr. Sanderson wouldn't know his trick had been discovered, but she couldn't stop running.

"Where have you been?" Jim demanded when he saw her. "Every time I turn around, you're gone! We were just about to launch a search."

She gasped for breath, then took his arm. Dragging him away from the others, who watched her with curiosity, she whispered frantically, "He's here! He's here!"

"Who's here?"

"Leroy Ferguson!"

"*What?*"

"Dr. Sanderson lied! I found the cave, and I saw Leroy Ferguson go inside! It's a trap!"

Jim gazed off down the trail. "He's *here*?"

"Yes!"

"You didn't leave Scout back there, did you?"

"Scout? What do you mean? She wasn't with me."

"Then where is she?"

"She was here when I left!" Anny frantically glanced around. Her sister's sleeping bag lay empty on the ground. "Where did she go?"

"I don't know, but we have to find her right away."

Panic swept over Anny. "What if she's in the cave?"

"She'd better not be..."

"She didn't pass me!"

"There might be another way to get there."

"We have to go get her!" Anny turned to run back down the trail, but Jim grabbed her arm.

"No! You can't go there!" Then he said gently, "Don't worry. I'll find her." He started leading her to the campfire. "Come on. We need to call the police and get you kids in the car. Then I'll get Scout."

Beside the fire, Ben and Eric were shaking out their sleeping bags.

"Forget your stuff," Jim told them. "Get in the car."

"What for?" asked Ben, as Jim reached into the front seat and pulled out his cell phone. "I thought we were going to look for the treasure when Anny and Scout got back."

Jim stared at the phone, pressed a button, then stared at the phone again. "A-a-agh! No service! Just when we need it most!" Throwing the phone onto the seat, he turned to Eric and Ben and began herding them toward the car.

Eric frowned at Jim. "What? What's happening?"

"No time for questions. Get in the car."

Dr. Sanderson stared at them as the two boys stood by the passenger doors to the station wagon and Anny lingered by the back door on the driver's side. "What's going on?"

Jim rested his hand on the open car door. "We're leaving."

"Why? What's wrong?"

"Look, we're on to your little plan. It won't work. Now I want you to tell him to let Scout go."

"Who?"

"As if you didn't know. Your pal Ferguson."

Dr. Sanderson scratched his head. "He's not my pal."

Jim shut the car door. "I don't want to play games," he snapped. "A child's life could be at stake. This is another kidnapping charge. I just want you to go with me to that cave and tell him to let her go."

"Cave?" Dr. Sanderson's eyes widened. "You mean he's here—in the cave? Are you sure?"

"I saw him! I want my sister back now!"

The color drained from Ben's face.

"Anny! What's happening?" cried Eric. "Tell me!"

"Oh, no...!" Dr. Sanderson looked genuinely shocked. "We made so much noise last night.... He must have heard us. And Dutch Turner must be with him, too." He paused. "I assure you I had nothing to do with this. Let's get these kids out of here. Then you and I can come back for Scout." He snatched up his hat from his sleeping bag and slapped it on.

"I'm not going anywhere without my sister!" Anny shouted. Knowing Scout was missing was like losing half of herself. She'd never been separated from her like this and it frightened her more than she ever could have imagined. "You'd better get her back right now!"

"Anny!" Eric shouted. "Tell me what's going on!"

"I'll do whatever I can," the archaeologist promised.

Jim looked at the archaeologist a moment. "You're denying that you knew Ferguson was coming here?"

"I had no idea, I swear. I wouldn't have brought you here if I had." He sighed. "What kind of a man do you think I am? You think I would put children in danger?"

"The problem is I don't really know." Jim got into the station wagon, then backed it up and turned it around so that it was facing toward the mountain highway. Then he rolled down the driver's window, fumbled with his cell phone, and got out. "Ben, you get in the driver's seat."

Ben slid behind the wheel, and Eric got in the passenger seat beside him. Anny climbed into the back seat, knowing she wasn't going to stay there. She was going with Jim and Dr. Sanderson to find her sister.

Jim closed the driver's door, then placed his hands on the sill of the open window and leaned into the car. "Okay, this is the deal. Dr. Sanderson and I are going after Scout. I have no choice but to trust him for the moment." He paused. "You need to drive down the mountain far enough for the cell phone to work. Then call Officer Yazzie. Just hit redial."

"We can't leave without you, Uncle Jim!" Ben cried.

Jim put a hand on Ben's shoulder. "I'll be fine. I need you to drive everyone to safety. Dr. Sanderson and I can leave in his SUV." He stood back from the car. "All set?"

Ben nodded, but from his tense expression, Anny knew he was as worried as she was. She quickly signed the entire story to a totally confused Eric, then turned around in her seat and watched through the rear window as Jim and Dr. Sanderson began walking up the trail to the cave.

Ben started the engine and the car rolled forward.

"Stop!" Anny shouted. "Let me out! I'm not leaving without my sister!"

Chapter 24

"You promised Jim you'd go with us," said Ben.

"I know, but—"

"Look!" The car lurched to a stop and Ben pointed a crooked finger out the windshield.

"What?" She leaned forward and gazed out the front window to see her sister ambling toward them. Anny leapt from the car and ran toward her, Ben and Eric right behind her.

"Scout!" She threw her arms around her sister and hugged her. "You're all right! I was so scared!"

Scout gently pushed her away. "Of course I'm all right. Why wouldn't I be?"

"Where were you?"

"I had to go to the bathroom. I wanted some privacy."

"It took that long?"

"I got sidetracked watching some birds."

"We thought Leroy Ferguson got you!"

"*What?*"

"Anny saw Leroy walk inside the cave!" said Eric. "We thought he caught you."

"Dr. Sanderson might have led us into a trap!" Anny added.

"Yeah!" said Ben. "And my uncle's walking right into it trying to rescue you." He turned to Anny. "How far is that cave, anyway? Can we catch them in time?"

"If we hurry."

"Let's go then. If Dr. Sanderson turns out to be a bad guy, my uncle will need our help."

"You have to call the police. They need to catch Dutch and Leroy before they get away again."

A stricken look crossed Ben's face.

"I wouldn't want to go either," Anny told him, "but you're the only one who can drive."

"Okay...," Ben reluctantly agreed. "You guys be careful." He got back into the driver's seat of the station wagon, shut the door, and started the engine. Then taking a deep breath, he put the car in gear and began rolling down the trail.

"Drive carefully!" Anny called after him as he disappeared through the trees. She still couldn't believe that a thirteen-year-old knew how to drive.

She broke into a run up the trail, Scout and Eric right behind her. Though she was panting and out of breath, she didn't stop until they got to the bend in the road. She gulped in air, then whispered as she signed, "It's up ahead. We have to sneak up on it."

Quietly they moved from tree to tree. No one was in sight. Even so, Anny was angry for not remembering to change into her gray sweatshirt. She stood out in the green and brown surroundings like a neon light. *Too late now*, she told herself.

In no time, they were in front of the cave entrance. Still, they saw no one.

"Jim and Dr. Sanderson must be inside," Anny whispered. "What do we do now?"

"Should we go in and check?" asked Eric.

"Oh, I don't know…," said Scout. "If we get caught, too, nobody can go for help."

"Let's just go in far enough to see if we hear voices," Anny suggested. "That poem said the treasure was fifty paces in. That's fifty steps, so they're probably in that far. They won't see us way back here."

Scout and Ben agreed, and they tiptoed to the low entrance. "You should wait here," Anny said to Scout. "Eric and I will go in. We can talk using sign language. No one will hear us."

"Okay…," Scout said, "but be careful."

Anny and Eric ducked as they entered the cave's mouth. Inside, they stood upright and stopped to allow their eyes to adjust to the dim light. The cave tunneled into darkness.

They had to walk only a few more feet before Anny heard voices echoing from far off down the musty passageway. She recognized Leroy Ferguson's voice and Dutch Turner's, too. *"I can hear them talking."* Panic gripped her. She had to go far enough into the cave to see if Jim and Dr. Sanderson were inside. She signed for Eric to wait while she checked. It would mean the risk of being seen, but she had no choice. She didn't feel both of them should chance being caught.

Her heart pounding wildly, she crept slowly along the passageway, her hands carefully feeling the cold sandy walls. She stopped every few steps to let her eyes adjust to the ever-growing darkness. Suddenly, a beam of light glowed from around a bend in the tunnel. She soon saw that the beam radiated from kerosene lanterns on the ground. Through it, she saw the back of the cave and the forms of Dutch Turner and Leroy Ferguson.

She wanted to run but forced herself to study the area carefully for any signs of Jim or Dr. Sanderson.

"They're all bound to come in here," Dutch Turner said confidently.

"When they do, we'll be ready." Leroy Ferguson's tone was menacing. "They wouldn't be here if that treasure wasn't in this cave. Nobody's taking it away from us."

"Those stupid kids think they're so smart. I still can't figure out how they got hooked up with the professor. He sure wouldn't help us."

"That old geezer'll pay when I get my hands on him. Just let him try to come in here."

Relieved that Dr. Sanderson was on their side and that he and Jim were not in the cave, Anny moved slowly back to Eric. Grabbing his arm, she signed in front of his face what she had seen. They quickly retreated outside.

"Dutch and Leroy are both in there," she whispered to Scout, "but they're alone."

"Then where are Jim and Dr. Sanderson?"

"I don't know. They must be looking someplace else. Dr. Sanderson is for real, just like he says. Dutch and Leroy plan to trap us when we go into the cave." Anny paused, looking at the large boulder beside her. It towered over their heads. "I have an idea. Let's roll this rock across the entrance. At least then Dutch and Leroy can't escape with the treasure."

"Roll that thing?" scoffed Scout. "It must weigh ten tons!"

"We have to try," Anny insisted.

Even with the three of them pushing together, heaving with all their might, they couldn't budge the massive boulder.

Scout leaned exhausted against it. "It's no use."

Then Anny saw him. He stood just behind them, smiling, his horse off in the distance, waiting patiently. The feathers that hung from his long, black hair were divided into uneven sections of red, yellow, and blue. The beads on the tops of his moccasins made little shapes of people and arrows in black, red, green, and yellow. Fringe trimmed the edges of his soft suede breechcloth, and his bow and arrows were slung over his shoulder. Anny saw the clay medallion clearly now. Carved on it was a thunderbird. She fingered hers, as if silently letting him know that she realized the two pieces of clay matched.

What had Mr. Roanhorse said? Anny asked herself. *The eyes are the windows to the soul.* She studied his dark face, his straight nose, his black eyes. They weren't hard and mean like Dutch Turner's. They were kind and gentle.

He pointed to himself, then made a pushing motion with his hands.

He wanted to help them move the boulder, Anny suddenly realized. Trusting her intuition, which gave her no uneasy feelings at the moment, she said, "Let's try once more."

"Oh, come on!" said Scout, a little too loudly. "It's impossible!"

"Sh-h-h-h!" Anny warned. "They'll hear you!" She took a deep breath. "Trust me, all right? Try it one more time."

Scout sighed, and just then, Anny saw the two treasure-hunters coming up the passageway to the cave entrance.

"Hey!" Dutch shouted, breaking into a run.

"Now!" Anny yelled. Together, the kids again pushed on the rock. The warrior stood behind them, his hands above theirs. This time, the rock rolled easily, and a moment later, it blocked the entrance, leaving an angry Dutch Turner and Leroy Ferguson shouting behind it.

"I don't believe it!" cried Eric.

"I don't, either!" echoed Scout.

"It was the warrior," Anny admitted, taking deep breaths to help her heart rate slow down. "He helped us."

"He's *here*?" cried Scout. "A ghost helped us?" Her eyes wild, she twirled around, looking for the phantom. "Where?"

Anny grabbed Scout's arm, trying to calm her down. She watched as the warrior returned to his horse, swung onto its back, then held up his hand to her. She did the same, smiling her thanks. He turned his horse and faded away as quickly as he had appeared. "He's gone now," she assured her sister.

"He'd better be! I don't want any of that ghost sickness Mrs. Roanhorse talked about."

"Don't worry," Anny said. "At least we have Dutch and Leroy where we want them until Officer Yazzie can get here."

"Now what?" asked Scout.

Anny sighed. "We wait, I guess. Jim and Dr. Sanderson should be back soon." At least she hoped they would.

No sooner had they returned to the campsite when Anny saw him again. The warrior sat astride his horse at the edge of the trees across the campsite. A slight smile on his dark face, he beckoned to her once again. She took hold of her sister's arm and whispered, "He's back...."

"Who? Ben?"

"No, the warrior...."

"The warrior?" Scout shrieked. "Where?"

"Over by the trees. He wants me to follow him."

"*What?* No!" Scout ran to Eric, who was rolling up his sleeping bag, and grabbed his arm. "The warrior wants Anny to follow him!"

Eric dropped the sleeping bag and ran to Anny, who turned her gaze back to the warrior.

"You can't!" he shouted. "It's too dangerous! You don't know if he's good or bad!"

Anny knew Eric and her sister were right to be suspicious. Though the phantom had helped them trap Dutch Turner and Leroy Ferguson in the cave, they couldn't be sure if he was looking out for them or trying to separate them from the adults.

Her parents had always said never to go anywhere with a stranger. They hadn't known she would be faced with a ghost.

"When you get separated from your group, you should stay in the spot where you last saw them," said Scout. "That means we should stay right here."

Anny hardly heard her sister. The warrior beckoned to her again, turned his horse toward the trees as if to leave, then turned back to her and beckoned yet again. She looked at Scout and Eric, remembering Mr. Roanhorse's words to trust her instincts. She knew that the warrior was not evil. "Let's all go."

Eric gasped. "You want us to follow a ghost?"

"No way!" Scout said flatly.

"Look, you know I wouldn't ask you to do anything dangerous. I don't get that weird feeling around him the way I do around Dutch and Leroy. Mr. Roanhorse told me to trust my instincts, and for once, I'm going to do it. They say that it's okay. I'm going, so you can stay here or come with me."

"I'm not staying here while you go who knows where!"

"Then come with me."

"Only under two conditions. We leave a note for Jim and we leave a trail of pine cones so that he and Dr. Sanderson can follow us as soon as they get here."

"Great idea." Anny thought again of Hansel and Gretel.

Scout took a pad and pen from her backpack, wrote a note to Jim, and placed it on a large rock. She put smaller rocks on top of it to hold it down. Then she put on her backpack. "Okay. I'm ready. I hope we're not making a big mistake."

After their night in the desert, Anny wasn't about to suggest that Scout leave the backpack behind, and she didn't think Eric would, either. She walked toward the warrior. *I'm following you,* she thought, hoping he would sense her words.

He turned his horse and the animal began moving through the trees up the mountain.

As Anny leaned forward to make it up the slope, she was grateful for her hiking boots. She began gasping for breath as they continued to climb for what seemed like an hour.

148

"How much farther?" complained Eric, huffing and puffing as Scout made another pile of pine cones.

"I don't know." Anny moved faster to keep up with the horse and rider.

They reached a wall of rock with a ledge high above. The warrior stopped, and so did Anny.

"What is it?" Scout asked.

Anny held up her hand for them to wait.

The warrior took an arrow from his quiver. Pointing his bow up the wall of rock, he shot the arrow over the ledge.

Anny stood dumbfounded.

"What? What?" Scout asked again.

Anny turned to face her and Eric. "I know where the treasure is."

Chapter 25

"What?" asked Eric. "Where?"

She pointed to the ledge. "Up there. The warrior shot an arrow over the edge." She craned her neck, trying to glimpse whatever was beyond the rocky shelf. Branches of tall pine trees shaded it.

"I don't see anything," said Scout.

"Whatever is up there, no one walking by can see it," she said, signing the words for Eric. "That must be what the warrior wants to show me—the location of the treasure."

"Why? And why *you*?"

Anny shrugged, continuing to study the ledge. "I don't know. It's just a feeling."

"There's no way to get up there to find out," said Eric.

"We could build a ladder," Scout suggested. Dropping her backpack on the ground, she looked around. "We need long, thick limbs for the sides and shorter, thinner ones for the rungs."

As they began searching for the required branches, Anny realized what a great team the three of them made. Scout's knowledge of the outdoors, Eric's sign language abilities, and her own strange powers were an unbeatable combination.

Tree limbs of all sizes littered the forest floor. After several minutes of searching, they had an arsenal of branches. One by one, Scout leaned the thick limbs against the rockface to see which ones were long enough to reach the top. When she had found two that extended above the ledge, she and Eric laid them out side by side on the ground.

"Now let's choose shorter branches to use as steps," Scout directed. When they had enough to make a ladder with rungs about a foot apart, they laid them in place.

"How do we tie them together?" asked Eric.

"With the rope I have in my backpack, of course."

"Boy, there really *is* something to that 'Be Prepared' stuff, isn't there?" he said in amazement.

"There sure is!" Scout unzipped the main compartment of the pack and retrieved a length of thin, coiled cord and a knife. "We'll have to cut this in sections. Unfortunately, if we need a long rope after that, we won't have one."

She carefully measured off several lengths and handed them to Anny and Eric. Taking one herself, she demonstrated how to lash it to the rungs and poles.

Anny and Eric immediately set to work, and soon the ladder was ready to test. Standing it up against the rock face, Scout put a foot on the first rung. She shifted her weight onto it and bounced lightly to see if it would hold her. With relief, Anny saw that it didn't budge.

Scout turned to Eric. "Hold the ladder while Anny and I go up there to check it out, okay?"

He nodded and put a hand on one side of the ladder.

"The warrior showed it to *you*," Scout said to Anny. "Want to go first?"

"Yeah!" Grasping the rough poles, Anny put one foot on the first rung. "Hold this ladder tight!"

"We will," Scout assured her. "Just be careful."

Anny moved her hands from rung to rung, recoiling briefly as her fingers struck some pitch on the back of one of them. Ignoring it and finding a pitch-free spot on the rung, she kept climbing until the ledge was at eye level. *One more step.* Pulling herself up yet again, she gasped. The low mouth of a cave was barely visible behind piles of scrub brush, twigs, and dead plant life. "I knew it!" she cried.

She stepped onto the ledge. Standing up, she gazed back down the mountain.

Eric waved to catch her attention. *"What do you see?"*

She signed as she spoke. "There's a cave up here! And straight across is a formation that looks like Window Rock. Behind it is a snowy peak!"

"The sun isn't quite overhead yet, but if this is the spot where the treasure is, then it's like we said. If we draw a line from the sun to the formation, the line making it a right angle, if it lines up with the snowy peak, will lead right to the spot where you're standing."

"I just know this is it!" She turned around and looked back at the cave. The entrance was only about three feet high. She would have to get on her hands and knees to fit through it. Picking up the accumulation of brush, she cast it down to the ground below.

When the opening was clear, she knelt beside it. She ignored the strange, musty odor wafting from inside as her gaze fell on a pictograph on the rocky surface in front of her. There was an image of the warrior on his horse, bow in hand, arrow drawn tautly toward her. Her excitement mounting, she recalled the next two lines of the poem. *The warrior at the secret lair, Get past his arrows if you dare.* She hoped he would let her pass, but she didn't dare enter the cave without Eric and her sister. It wouldn't be fair. They all should share in the discovery. Leaning over the edge of the stony shelf, she cried, "This is it! Just like the poem says! This is it!"

On the ground, Eric held the ladder for Scout. When she reached the ledge, she and Anny held it for him. On hands and knees, they crawled through the low hole. Inside, the cave was large enough for them to stand up.

Brushing dirt from her hands and the knees of her jeans, Anny let her eyes adjust to the darkness. She reeled backwards, crashing into Scout and Eric, as a shadowy form appeared in front of her.

Chapter 26

"What happened?" Scout yelled.

"What's wrong?" cried Eric.

"Somebody's there!" Anny tried to shout, but she couldn't speak. The dark form suddenly took shape, and she realized it was the warrior. He held his bow in one hand. *He isn't going to stop us now, is he? Is he evil, after all?* Anny took several deep breaths, trying to raise the fifty-pound weight that seemed to be crushing her chest.

Suddenly, the cave glowed with soft, golden light.

"What's that?" Eric gasped, glancing around. "Where's that light coming from?"

Anny finally found her voice. "You can see that?" she said and signed.

"Yes," answered Eric.

"So can I," said Scout.

The warrior smiled, not in a sinister manner but a friendly one. Then he gestured down the passageway as though telling them their path was clear.

Anny sighed with relief. "It's the warrior. He wants us to walk through the cave." The poem had warned, "Get past his arrows if you dare." She took a tentative step forward. The warrior backed up and again gestured down the passageway. She smiled back at him. She just knew he was showing them where the treasure was!

With growing confidence in her ability to understand his wishes, she said to the others, "Our feet are probably smaller than those of the man who wrote the poem, so our fifty paces may not get us exactly to the right spot, but it'll be close."

Taking a deep breath, she began to count as she walked, Scout and Eric right behind her. "One...two...three...." The glowing light the warrior provided followed them as they walked, offering perfect visibility.

When Anny reached fifty, she stopped. "It has to be right around here." She froze.

Eric and Scout crashed into her.

They all screamed.

Chapter 27

A human skeleton lay scattered several feet away. Scout's nails sank into Anny's arm, but she hardly noticed; her nails were sinking just as deeply into Eric's. Gently, Eric removed her hand, then took a step forward, his arms outstretched to shield her and Scout.

"Who-o-o's th-a-a-a-t?" her sister stammered.

Anny finally found her voice. "D-d-d-on't know...."

Eric turned to them. "I'll bet that's somebody who tried to get the treasure and the warrior's arrows got him."

He hadn't heard her and Scout speak, Anny thought, but he had come up with a good assumption. *Has the warrior tricked us into coming this far into the cave so he could kill us, too?* "I don't see any arrows anywhere...," Anny managed to say and sign.

"He's a ghost, remember? His arrows aren't of this world."

Shaking, Anny and Scout stood staring for several more moments at the yellowed bones.

"Look...."

Anny tore her gaze away to see Scout pointing to a depression in the ground. She slowly untangled her sister's fingers from her arm and slid sideways, away from the skeleton, to study it closer. "Fifty paces down you'll walk to see the sun upon the rock.... I'll bet the Magic Rock was right here.... Then dig beneath that golden sun, and Spanish treasure you'll have won. This has to be it!" She quickly signed her theory to Eric.

Eric nodded toward the skeleton. "Given what happened to that poor guy, do you really want to dig for it? I'm all for getting out of here." He paused. "Anyway, remember what Jim said. You need the Tribal Council's permission."

"Jim will help us get it," Anny found herself saying. *Has the warrior put a spell on* me *this time?* she wondered. *Am I crazy to think about still digging for treasure when someone who has obviously tried it is lying dead not ten feet away? Does the warrior want* us *dead, too?*

Suddenly, she heard voices calling their names. "That sounds like Ben and Jim!"

"Yeah!" Scout said with relief. "No need to mark the spot. The skeleton's done that for us."

The three rushed to the front of the cave and scrambled to the ledge. Ben, Jim, Dr. Sanderson, Officer Yazzie, and two other Tribal Police officers, one a woman, stood at the base of the ladder, gazing up at them.

"My pine cone trail worked!" exclaimed Scout.

They descended the ladder.

"You're going to be the death of me yet!" said Jim. "Are you all right?"

"Fine, now that you're here!" Scout said. "Wait til you hear what we found!"

Anny could hardly believe how happy she was to be among adults again. "There's a skeleton up there!" The whole story came spilling out, and she didn't stop until she got to the end.

"We need the FBI on this one," said Officer Yazzie.

"I should be able to tell whether it's a modern crime scene, Officer," said Dr. Sanderson.

"We think this is the cave where the Magic Rock came from," said Scout.

"You haven't been digging, have you?" Dr. Sanderson asked, in a worried tone.

"No way!" Scout assured him. "We don't want to end up like that skeleton! The warrior got him good!"

"My guess is that the pothunter I mentioned is responsible." The archaeologist shook his head. "Greed...."

Anny didn't respond. She just knew the warrior had stopped whoever had tried to take the treasure, and he was probably the one who had made the pothunter go crazy in the desert. Her heart leapt into her throat. *What if the pothunter had dug up the treasure and lost it somewhere? Just because he had the Magic Rock didn't mean that that was all he had taken!*

"Where did you go?" Scout asked Jim. "We were sure you were in the cave with Dutch and Leroy."

"We looked inside, but no one was there. We assumed Dutch had to be nearby, so we decided to take a lesson from Ben and look for his truck to disable it. We didn't want them getting away again."

"They were both in there when we looked," said Anny. She explained how she and Eric had seen them in the cave.

158

Eric's face beamed. "And they're *still* in there!"

"They were setting a trap for all of us," said Scout. "We rolled a boulder across the front of the cave to trap them!"

"You did what?" asked Jim.

"We rolled a boulder across the mouth of the cave," Anny repeated.

"How in the world...?" said Officer Yazzie.

"We had some help...," Anny admitted.

"From whom?" asked Jim.

Anny glanced at Scout and Eric.

"Go ahead. Tell him," said Scout.

Anny swallowed. "The warrior. The warrior helped us."

"Warrior?" asked Officer Yazzie. "What warrior?"

"The one from the poem," said Scout. "He guards the treasure."

"I have a pretty hard time believing that story," said Jim. He threw his arms in the air. "What am I saying? At this point, I think I'd believe anything!"

"We'll get to the bottom of that later," said Officer Yazzie. "It's time we arrested those men."

Back at the cave, the adults stared at the boulder covering its entrance. They shook their heads.

"I don't understand how you did that," said Officer Yazzie. "It'll take all of us to move it."

"We can do it," said Anny. "We rolled it before."

"Thanks," he said, "but those men may have guns. I don't want you kids in the line of fire when we confront them. We'll do it."

Anny, Eric, Scout, and Ben hid safely behind some trees—with strict orders not to move—as Jim, Dr. Sanderson, and two of the officers positioned themselves beside the boulder.

Officer Yazzie stood back, his gun drawn. "Okay, push now," he told them.

With tremendous effort, they rolled the rock away from the cave's entrance, then Jim and Dr. Sanderson leapt out of the way as Officer Yazzie rushed forward into the cave. Quickly, the other two officers drew their guns and followed him inside.

Shortly, they heard Turner and Ferguson yelling, and a moment later, Officer Yazzie emerged from the cave pushing a handcuffed Dutch Turner in front of them. The other two officers followed with Leroy Ferguson.

Anny jumped out from behind the tree. "I was right! You *were* treasure-hunting! And now you're going to jail!"

Turner glared at her. "Yeah? So are you for having your Indian friend and his horse try to run us down." He turned to Officer Yazzie. "I want to file charges against these kids!"

Anny smiled to herself. So the two criminals *had* seen the warrior!

"Never mind that," said Officer Yazzie, pushing his prisoner ahead of him. "They've done nothing wrong."

"Stupid brats!" Turner spat. "Why didn't you mind your own business?"

"That's enough," said Yazzie. "They deserve a medal."

"Just one question," Jim said to Dutch Turner. "Why did you burn down the school?"

Turner's eyes widened, then narrowed. "I don't know what you're talking about."

"We know you did it," Jim went on, "so you might as well confess. Those gas cans gave you away. And Anny found your headband where you were digging under the building. Why'd you do it?"

Turner was silent a moment. "That poem said the treasure was beneath the golden sun. We thought for sure it was under that rock—which meant under the school."

"You fools! That rock was moved there twenty-five years ago."

"How were we supposed to know that?" Leroy Ferguson broke in.

"But why the fire?" Jim persisted.

"To cover the holes we dug," said Turner. "We figured no one would notice them with all the mess."

"And you helped clean up because...?"

"Just in case the treasure really was there."

"That's why you dug two more holes?"

"Just wanted to be sure," said Turner.

When they reached the campsite, the officers put Turner into the back seat of one squad car and Ferguson into the back seat of another and drove away.

Jim turned to Anny and the others. "Well, kids, if those bones prove to be ancient, we'll need permission to do some digging."

Chapter 28

The next morning, they had their answer. The Tribal Council had met the night before and granted permission for digging under the watchful eyes of Dr. Sanderson and Officer Yazzie. The skeleton was not to be touched if Dr. Sanderson suspected it resulted from a modern crime.

"If it is," Jim said, "Officer Yazzie has to call in the FBI. Then we can't do any digging until they finish their investigation—maybe not even then."

"What if it's an ancient site?" asked Anny, not sure at all that she wanted to hear the answer if it was more bad news.

Jim said. "The Tribal Council will make arrangements for a proper burial, just in case the person was an Indian. The remains are not to be disturbed, and any digging can be done only in places away from it."

No problem, Anny thought. The skeleton was several feet away from the suspected original location of the Magic Rock. She kept her fingers crossed that he or she wouldn't turn out to be someone the pothunter had killed. "Your father has to be there," she told Jim. "Without him, we wouldn't even know about the legend."

"Now remember," he said. "Don't get your hopes up. As I said before, even if there was a treasure, it was probably looted long ago." All the same, he agreed that his father would enjoy following the clues, if he felt up to climbing the mountain.

Anny tried not to let his negativity dampen her mood as they drove to Mr. Roanhorse's hogan and then to the mountains, the archaeologist following in his SUV. Officer Yazzie met them at the campsite.

Anny's excitement grew as they got shovels, kerosene lanterns, and other gear from Dr. Sanderson's truck and hauled everything to the cave. She knew Eric, Ben, and Scout shared her exhilaration.

"I cannot climb that ladder, my son," said Mr. Roanhorse, who was exhausted from the long hike. "I will wait here."

Anny was sad that he wouldn't be there to witness the digging, but she understood. She remembered what he had said about ghost sickness. She knew he didn't want to be around the remains of a dead person.

On the ledge, Jim lit the lanterns, which he, Dr. Sanderson, and Officer Yazzie carried inside the dark cavern.

Where was the warrior? Anny wondered as they headed down the passageway. Soon they reached the skeleton. Anny hung back behind Jim as the men studied it.

"Well, Dr. Sanderson?" asked Officer Yazzie.

Anny held her breath, crossing her fingers behind her back.

The archaeologist swung the lantern slowly over the area. "This isn't a modern crime scene. That skeleton has been here a very long time."

"Then we can start digging?" Anny asked.

"Not yet," the archaeologist replied. "We have to separate this area so no one disturbs it." He set the lantern on the ground, pulled some stakes from a bag, and roped off the skeleton behind a string fence.

Anny pointed to her left. "I think that's the spot where the Magic Rock came from."

She didn't think she could stand it as Dr. Sanderson photographed the area and pounded the stakes into the cave floor several feet apart to make a six-foot by six-foot square. Then he tied string to the stakes in both directions to create smaller squares.

"Now we can we start digging," he said.

Jim held out a shovel to Anny. "Would you like to be first?"

She took it, then shrieked, "I'm digging for buried treasure!"

Jim placed a hand on her shoulder. "Remember, there may be nothing here."

She nodded, but she was ready to dig clear to China before she would give up looking.

After she had dug several scoops in the hard-packed sand, Scout, Eric, and Ben had a turn, then Jim and Officer Yazzie took over. Dr. Sanderson held a clipboard and pencil, ready to record whatever they found. He halted the digging every few minutes to take measurements.

When they had dug about two feet, Jim stopped. "Sorry, kids, I don't think there's anything here."

"Keep going!" cried Anny. "Please!"

Jim turned to Dr. Sanderson. "What do you think?"

The archaeologist sighed, and Anny held her breath, terrified that the man would end their adventure at the drop of a word. "Well, we've found things in digs a lot deeper than this one," he said. "I agree with Anny. We should keep going—a few more feet, anyway."

Relief swept over Anny, and she swallowed as she looked at the others, who stood wide-eyed, staring at the men.

They had dug another two feet when Jim's shovel suddenly stopped with a loud thud.

Anny gasped. "You've hit something!"

Dr. Sanderson quickly knelt down and dropped a tape measure into the hole.

It was all Anny could do to keep herself from jumping into the pit and scooping up dirt with her hands.

"Okay," he said, setting the tape measure down and scribbling on his clipboard. "Go ahead."

Jim smiled at Anny and then looked at the archaeologist. "Okay if she takes over from here?"

"Be my guest."

With a cheer, Anny dropped into the hole and fell to her knees. She began scooping up dirt furiously with her hands. A few moments later, a curved, brown, wooden surface peered through the dirt. "It looks like the top of something!"

Dr. Sanderson took more of his aggravating measurements and pictures, then Anny dug feverishly, and with everyone's help, they freed a trunk-like box from its earthly prison and set it on the ground beside them.

"I don't believe it!" exclaimed Jim. "Never in a million years would I have expected to find anything here!"

Jim and Officer Yazzie helped the kids lift the old chest to the cave floor as Dr. Sanderson photographed it again.

"It sure feels heavy enough," said Jim.

"Could be filled with dirt," said Dr. Sanderson. He removed a soft brush from his pack and began cleaning the trunk.

Anny climbed out of the pit. *We've finally found the treasure and you want to clean it off? I can't stand it!*

"That wood is in remarkably good condition after being buried this long," said Jim.

Who cares about the wood? Let's see what's inside of it!

Dr. Sanderson continued brushing. "These caves are so dry that most perishable materials are very well preserved."

As the sand fell away, two old, worn, leather straps, brittle with age, appeared, nailed around the box. Their buckles were dull. Pieces of hammered metal covered the corners of the lid and bottom, and thin strips of it were nailed several inches apart where the sides met the front and back. A large clasp adorned the front, and from it hung a large padlock.

"That looks just like a pirate treasure chest!" said Eric.

"It sure does!" agreed Ben.

"Let's open it at the front of the cave where we can see better," said Dr. Sanderson.

"No!" Anny said. "Let's open it down below so Mr. Roanhorse can see!"

Everyone agreed. Anny had waited this long to see what was in the box. She thought she could wait a little longer.

At the cave mouth, where there was enough room to stand and enough light to see, they set down the chest. Using a rope of Dr. Sanderson's, the archaeologist and Jim carefully lowered the trunk down the cliff. Mr. Roanhorse stood at the ladder's base, guiding it to the ground. Then they lowered the shovels and other gear and took turns descending the ladder.

When they were standing together again, Dr. Sanderson pulled a thin metal rod from his equipment and began to pick the lock. "I hope I can do this without breaking it."

He worked on it for several minutes. Finally, it fell open. Then he removed the lock, gently flipped up the latch, and opened the lid. Granules of sand that had found their way between the lid and the bottom crumbled to the ground.

Anny could hardly believe her eyes! The chest wasn't filled with dirt. Inside were thousands of gold coins and red, green, and blue jewels. On top rested a hefty, jewel-encrusted, golden cross and a large, round, clay medallion with a thunderbird stamped in its center. She and the others stared, speechless.

Jim picked up the golden cross. "Would you look at this...? There really *is* a treasure!"

Anny held the clay medallion gently. "This belongs to the warrior," she said quietly.

"Rubies, sapphires, and emeralds!" Dr. Sanderson picked up some gold coins and turned them over in his hand. "And Spanish doubloons!" He paused. "As I recall, the Garza family has offered a sizable reward for finding that cross."

"I know," said Anny. "They have to get it back. The reward should go to the Navajo Nation to rebuild the school."

"Unreal," said Officer Yazzie. "I would never have believed it. We'd better get this box back to Window Rock."

Suddenly she saw the warrior, sitting calmly on his horse at the edge of the woods. Leaving Ben, Eric, and Scout oogling the treasure with the men, she moved toward him, watching him intently, wondering what she should say, if anything.

Mr. Roanhorse followed her, and Jim was right behind him.

"He's back," she whispered. "The warrior is back...."

"Ah, yes," the old man said, watching the rider intently. "So he is...."

Anny held her breath. "Then you see him." It was a statement, not a question.

Jim followed their gaze. "I see him, too...."

"What?" cried Anny. "You *can*?"

"Yes. All my years of scientific training.... I never would have believed...." His voice trailed off.

Mr. Roanhorse nodded. "Mm. Mm." He nodded again. "I understand."

"Understand what?" asked Anny. She hadn't heard the warrior say anything.

"I understand his story," the old man said, "his purpose in all of this."

"What did he say?"

Mr. Roanhorse took a deep breath. "He has waited a long time for this day. It is not good to speak of the dead and how a person died, but he wants you to know. He was living in the cave when Diego Garza came with his treasure. Garza killed him so that he could use the cave to hide the fortune. The skeleton you found is his. At the same time, Garza stole his medallion. The warrior's spirit vowed that he would never let anyone as greedy as Diego Garza find the treasure."

"Why did he show it to me?" Anny asked.

"Because you had an honorable goal for its use. You wanted to give it to the *Diné*, not keep it for yourself. He wants the tribe to have his medallion and to keep it safe with the Magic Rock."

"He said all that?" Anny replied. "Why didn't he talk to me?"

"He says you must learn more before you speak to spirits."

"And why did he show himself to me?" Jim asked.

"In your heart, you know, my son," Mr. Roanhorse answered.

"I suppose I do...," Jim said quietly. "So I would believe in the old ways again."

"His time of guarding the secret lair is over," Mr. Roanhorse said. "At last, he can go home to the Great Spirit. He thanks you, Anny."

The phantom held up his hand to her in farewell.

"I don't even know your name," she said to him.

"Tee-wa-nee-ka," said Mr. Roanhorse. "His name is Tee-wa-nee-ka."

The warrior turned his horse and faded away among the trees.

Ghapter 29

Anny, Scout, Eric, and Ben stepped out of the station wagon in front of Windy Mesa School. Today, Jim was taking them back to Phoenix so she, Scout, and Eric could catch their flight to California and Ben could return home.

The week went by so fast, Anny thought. *I'm sorry to be leaving.*

They had planned a terrific science fair for Windy Mesa. Mrs. Nakai had asked them to meet her in her office on their way to the airport, and Mr. Roanhorse had followed them in Jim's red pickup.

The principal came rushing out of the wrought-iron gates to meet them. "I'm so glad you're here!" she said, a big smile lighting up her face.

"She's sure excited about *something*," Scout whispered to her, and Anny agreed, eagerly wondering what it was.

Mrs. Nakai ushered them inside to her office. File folders stood in neat piles on the gray metal desk, and two wooden chairs with green pads stood in front of it.

The principal picked up one of the folders and took a deep breath, the smile never leaving her face. Anny noticed that

Jim, Ben, and Mr. Roanhorse were smiling, too. *Ben had known all along about this!* she thought.

"Well! A lot has happened this week," she began. "You found the lost treasure, and Dutch Turner and Leroy Ferguson are safely behind bars. And you helped Dr. Sanderson bury Tee-wa-nee-ka in his cave."

Anny thought about the prayers Mr. Roanhorse had said outside the cave to help the warrior go to the Great Spirit. *I hope he made it okay.*

"The treasure arrived safely at the University of Arizona to be catalogued," the principal went on. "Soon it will be in a museum for everyone to enjoy." She paused. "That leads me to why I asked you to come here today. As you know, we sent the cross back to the Garzas by overnight mail. They wired us the reward money on one condition—that each of you keeps five thousand dollars."

Anny and the others gasped in unison.

Mrs. Nakai handed each of them a cashier's check.

Anny's hands shook as she stared at hers in disbelief. "But won't you need all the money to rebuild the school?" she found herself saying.

"You've been generous enough," said Jim. "Besides, as Mrs. Nakai said, this was the Garzas' idea. They wouldn't send the reward unless we agreed."

"And the remaining $80,000 is safely in the bank in a building fund account," Mrs. Nakai added.

"Now it is my turn," said Mr. Roanhorse, holding out his hands.

171

Mrs. Nakai handed him the folder. "We wanted to find some way to thank you for everything you've done for our school. Mr. Roanhorse came up with the perfect answer."

The elderly man cleared his throat. "The Tribal Council has agreed to make you—Anny, Scout, and Eric—honorary members of our tribe." He handed each of them a parchment certificate with colorful lettering, a gold seal in one corner, and their names in large black letters in the middle.

"Oh, wow!" Anny studied hers carefully. "This is so cool!"

"Yes, it is!" said Scout. "Wait 'til my Girl Scout leader sees this!"

"My grandma will really be surprised!" Eric added.

"I've got one more thing," said Jim. "Your new name. From now on, I'm calling you four The Phantom Hunters!"

KIDS! PARENTS! TEACHERS!

Look for Book #2 in *The Phantom Hunters™* series:

The Secret of Wentworth House

When Anny's and Scout's grand-father dies, their family is stunned to learn they have inherited a man-or house on the Yorkshire moors in England. They didn't even know Grandpa had owned Wentworth House. Eager to see the place, the twins, their younger brother, Jordan, and their parents, along with their friends, Ben Lapahie and Eric Larson, take a trip to the village of Blackhurst. They are even more stunned when all they find is a pile of rubble. Why had their grandfather left them this wreck? Why hadn't he warned them so they wouldn't take a trip halfway around the world for nothing? What had happened to Wentworth House? These questions swirl in Anny's head. Once again, she is getting that creepy feeling. Something is not right. The mysterious family that appears outside her room at the inn is only the beginning.

Go to www.phantomhunters.com to:

Join The Phantom Hunters Club!
Download great science projects, games, and other fun stuff!

TEACHERS!

Check out www.phantomhunters.com for teacher re-sources to accompany this book series and other kids' books by Stargazer Publishing Company.

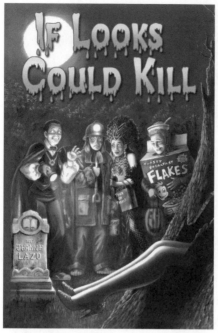

Fourteen might be too old for trick-or-treating in some towns, but not in The Village of Dorseyville, Pennsylvania, a rural hamlet just slightly south of Nowhere. Living in a place where nothing ever happens, I pretty much know what to expect in any situation.

On Halloween night, I expected my best friend, Fawn Flodi, to dress up like a model; I expected Art Zampini to melt me with his good looks while annoying me no end with his constant teasing; I expected Tucker Riggoli to happily disappear inside of his cereal box costume; and I could have bet my library card that none of us would fill our bags with candy.

But I didn't expect to go into Pinecreek Presbyterian Cemetery and stumble upon a woman's body stuffed inside of the hollow Death Tree, wearing red shoes with four-inch high heels, toes pointing up to the dark heavens. Murder...it's enough to make me want to move.

A week later, the same red shoes reappeared in a painting on display in the window of the Aspinwall Art Gallery. Fawn and I freaked when we saw it. Why would someone paint old Mrs. Glassport wearing those shoes? She'd never own a pair like that! The whole thing reeked of something sinister.

My name is Priggs, short for Priscilla Griggs, and that body and those red shoes were just the beginning of my spine-chilling ordeal.

Ages 10 and up   160 pages   5½" x 8½" $14.95

ISBN: 0-9713756-4-X Hardcover

STARGAZER
Publishing Company
PO Box 77002
Corona, CA 92877-0100
"Educate, Enlighten, Empower"

www.stargazerpub.com